Panda Books

A World of Dreams

Lu Wenfu, a vice-chairman of the Chinese Writers' Association, was born on March 23, 1928. In late spring of 1944 he went to Suzhou, where he spent three years at secondary school and fell in love with that beautiful, ancient city with its rich natural and cultural endowments.

After finishing school he joined guerrillas fighting foreign aggression and oppressive rule. It was on the eve of Liberation, and the Kuomintang government collapsed before he had fought a single battle. He returned to Suzhou with the army and worked as a journalist on the *Suzhou Daily*.

His first story, *Honour*, appeared in *Literary Monthly* in the early fifties and was favourably reviewed. He joined the East China branch of the Chinese Writers' Association. His next story, *Deep Within a Lane*, caused a sensation, and he became a professional writer in Nanjing in the spring of 1957.

Disaster struck with the anti-Rightist movement that began soon after. Lu was sent back to Suzhou to work in a machine plant until the summer of 1960, when he was transferred back to Nanjing and creative writing.

The "cultural revolution" intervened. He was sent to work as a mechanic in a cotton mill and then farmed for nine years.

After the "cultural revolution" he returned to Suzhou and resumed his writing career.

Lu Wenfu

A World of Dreams

Panda Books

Panda Books
First edition 1986

ISBN 0-8351-1601-8

Published by CHINESE LITERATURE, Beijing (37), China
Distributed by China International Book Trading Corporation
(GUOJI SHUDIAN), P.O. Box 399, Beijing, China
Printed in the People's Republic of China

CONTENTS

A Weak Light 7

Deep Within a Lane 17

Tang Qiaodi 41

The Man from a Pedlars' Family 66

The Boundary Wall 89

The Gourmet 121

The Doorbell 215

A World of Dreams 236

A Weak Light

IF you look at it from a certain angle, writing isn't really a good profession since writers are forever torturing themselves. This world is never as writers would wish it to be, nor are human souls entirely as writers portray them. Yet they constantly overrate their own abilities and diligently toil away, burning their hearts' blood to emit a weak light. They are seldom content, seldom composed, and drive themselves relentlessly, their anxieties outweighing their consolations, experiencing extreme emotions that sometimes even breed crises.

I had a lot of wonderful aspirations when I was young, but none of them was to become a writer. This isn't to say that I saw it as a bad profession. On the contrary, I thought people who could write books were terrific — if they weren't actually gods, then they at least inhabited the same terrain. When I was seven I started to study the works of Confucius, and even my teacher bowed before the sage's tablet. From childhood onwards my imagination was prone to run wild. Imagination is always closely tied to literature, which can give a child's mind an accessible and limitless universe.

Imagination needs inducement and my first inducement was a great river — the Yangtse. I was born on March 23, 1928 in a small village on its north bank. The river was only two hundred metres from my house and every day I was woken up and lulled to sleep by the sound of its rolling waves. Every day I sat gazing out from the dyke, watching boats heave into view on the horizon and then disappear slowly again into the distance. This aroused a wonder about what the world was really like. But I couldn't quite imagine. Looking eastwards there was water and sky, to the west sky and water, a vast blank expanse which couldn't fully nurture my daydreams.

When literature came into my life, it made my imagination take root and develop. It gave me a multifaceted world in which there were monsters and fairies, then love and friendship, happiness and tears, dastardly deeds and noble acts, robbery and righteousness. I was totally bewitched and wanted to experience all of this myself. But none of these things happened in my village, nor in the small county town where I went to school. The most distant settings were faraway lands, the closest Shanghai, Nanjing and Suzhou. Suzhou I could get to; my aunt had a shop there.

In late spring of 1944, I arrived in Suzhou wearing a long gown and a hat. Always known as a paradise on earth, it was even more beautiful than I had imagined. Like history or classical poetry, it was the source of all kinds of beautiful stories. In a way, I seemed to have read them already. A young man who had toured the world in his imagination had finally found a resting place. I stayed to spend three years there at secondary school and have loved the city ever since.

At the end of that three years I realized that Suzhou was like a beautiful lake, that it had a lot of dirt beneath its clear surface. The city had a lot of beautiful women but many of them rode in rickshaws pulled by emaciated, gasping old men. In those years of corrupt and incompetent Kuomintang rule, Suzhou's beautiful exterior could no longer hide its people's sufferings. My interest and imagination turned to society, to fighting for a better social system so that its people could live in a real paradise.

After graduation, I didn't go to college and left instead to join the guerrilla forces. But before I fought a single battle the Kuomintang collapsed. I went back to Suzhou with the army and worked as a journalist on the *Suzhou Daily* for eight years, during which time our country made great progress. I warmly praised the new order in reports, articles and commentaries. But this kind of journalism didn't satisfy me, for it was based purely on fact and made me feel as if I had something stuck in my throat. I suddenly decided to try my hand at writing stories. Though based on real life, they could still be fictitious. Imagination could bring an artistic perfection to fact. By this time I no longer considered writers sages, for a writer and a journalist were not that different. I was twenty-five then, and fairly quick off the mark. To be honest, I thought of writing fiction partly to praise the new society, partly for the fun of it and partly to gain the limelight. It certainly never occurred to me that writing could turn out to be a dangerous game.

I worked morning till night for over a month writing a story which I sent to the *Literary Monthly* in Shanghai. This first attempt wasn't accepted, but the kind editor wrote a three-page letter saying that my writing showed promise and encouraging me to continue. I liked compliments in those days (now I'm rather wary of them) and was spurred by this editor's opinion to make another attempt. My next story, *Honour*, was given a prominent spot in *Literary Monthly* and was accompanied by a complimentary review. There weren't that many short-story writers then, and this piece turned me into a writer and a member of the East China branch of the Chinese Writers' Association. I went to its first national conference of young writers in Beijing and met a lot of the people who made their names in the fifties and are now quite distinguished. After that I couldn't stop. I published another story, *Deep Within a Lane*, which caused a sensation because most of the stories then were about fighting, production, model workers and military heroes while mine was about the life and love of a prostitute, about humanism, and was written in fine language. According to the contemporary vernacular, it was full of petty bourgeois sentiment. In the spring of 1957, when a professional writers' group was established under the Jiangsu branch of the Federation of Literary and Art Circles, it recruited people who had made some headway in literature in the province. I was no longer a journalist and became a professional writer in Nanjing.

It had never really occurred to me that I would be a professional writer, but now I had to give the idea some consideration: what was it that a writer actually did, what were his responsibilities towards society, what should he write and how? With me were Gao Xiaosheng, the late Fang Zhi, Ai Xuan, Ye Zhicheng, Mei Rukai and Chen Chunnian. We put our heads together and decided that literature ought not only to praise, it should intrude on life in all its aspects and should use creative methods other than socialist realism. It should be about people and should look at the course of human events rather than be about political policies and movements. We also felt that excessive class struggle had already destroyed normal human relationships and shattered the fabric of our social life. These views — acceptable now — were outrageous twenty-eight years ago. Yet we not only stated them verbally, we decided to publish a magazine called *Explorers* to realize our views through art. We wrote a foreword expounding our ideas, but before the magazine was published the 1957 anti-Rightist movement began. Calamity befell us. We became an anti-Party clique and were criticized, struggled against, asked to examine our thinking and sent out of the city. Chen was sent to a labour farm, Gao back to his village, Ai to work in an orchard in the Western Hills, Fang and Ye to a steel mill. I was ordered to return to Suzhou to be an apprentice in a machine plant. None of us came out to the good. This was the "Explorers' Incident", notorious in Chinese cultural circles in the fifties. After less than half a year of the writer's life, I tumbled right down into the abyss. Writing was hardly a wonderful career.

I worked at a lathe for two years, during which time I genuinely learned a great deal from my fellow workers. Like writers, they were human beings, yet their laborious and also creative work was totally unsung. There was a lot for intellectuals to learn from. In those days, life was hard for a Rightist or an anti-Party element; if you saw a friend you didn't dare acknowledge one another. But workers didn't pay attention to that sort of thing, and provided you were honest and hardworking, they befriended you and secretly sympathized with you. They praised my hard work and I even won several prizes, including a track suit and a large enamel basin. Good fortune hadn't entirely forsaken me in my disaster. Yet this good fortune harboured misfortune too; who could define what was good and what was bad....

In the summer of 1960, after the three years of natural disasters, an economic readjustment took place and the cultural world came back to life. A professional writing group was set up again in Jiangsu Province. Since my work at the factory had been outstanding enough to indicate that my reformation had been successful, I was transferred to Nanjing to be a professional writer again. My tumble had sharpened my wits. I became extremely careful and knew my place. But it was hard to write stories when class struggle was foremost. All the heroes were robust giants, three or four times bigger than ordinary people. I couldn't really fall in with this, because I was only 1.74 metres tall and had never seen such giants myself. Maybe they existed up in heaven, but I had never even been on a plane. So I wrote about ordinary labourers, about their work and about their outlook. From my more than two years in the factory, I broke fresh ground in my work and was quite prolific. I once again attracted attention in the literary world and got a lot of complimentary reviews. Wasn't that wonderful? Wait.

In 1964 when the economy picked up a bit, class struggle began again. Writers and artists became more and more tense and writing became difficult. Anxious, the heads of the Writers' Association convened a meeting in Beijing to discuss which approaches to literature were most suitable. The meeting was attended by Mao Dun and other famous writers and literary theoreticians. I was present too. Mao Dun expressed a lot of interest in my stories, saying that they indicated a promising future. The review he published in the *Literary Gazette* couldn't have come at a worse time, though, for literature and art were being criticized for their revisionist tendencies. And who was Lu Wenfu? On investigation I was discovered to be one of the 1957 "explorers" — an anti-Party element. The appearance of such a person on the literary scene was itself an expression of class struggle. I had to be denounced.

This time I really got it; the attacks were much more severe than in 1957 and went on for six whole months. A lot of newspapers carried condemnations. Two whole pages in a Jiangsu newspaper were devoted to long articles about me. I was totally bewildered. It seemed only the day before I had been praised for my writing and now I was suddenly accused of being anti-Party and anti-socialist. Was this reasonable? Of course, those who criticized me (they were only carrying out orders) gave their reasons, claiming that I depicted mediocre characters, that I talked about the dark side of society and about humanism instead of class struggle, and that I still clung to my views as an "explorer". My new errors as well as my old 1957 ones were jointly denounced. At first they couldn't convince me I was in the wrong but later, overcome by despair, I almost threw myself off the Linggu Temple. In the end I didn't, stopped by a desire to see what would happen to literature and art. I couldn't write any more, nor did I want to; I only wanted to watch. In the summer of 1965 I was kicked out of the literary world again, back to Suzhou where I became a mechanic in a cotton mill. I didn't read or write; I just drank half a bottle of wine a day and hummed the *Song of Lake Baikal*, written in the days when the Chinese Red Army had been forced to retreat across the Soviet border. My tearful hoarse voice always drove my children out of the house. During the "cultural revolution" I had an even harder time. I was struggled against, forced to confess my crimes and paraded through the streets with a placard around my neck. I myself was already numb to the pain, and only worried about when this disaster for my country would end. Every step socialism made was difficult, while destruction was so easy. When would that happy society I had dreamt of as a boy be realized? A worker could always make a living by working. But they wouldn't even let me be a worker for long and told me to go off and be a peasant. In late 1969, my whole family was sent to the countryside and we had to leave Suzhou with five days' notice. A person who had dreamt of building up that paradise was once again banished from it.

My wife and I and our two daughters went to the Yellow Seacoast, the poorest part of Jiangsu, known to the banished as the Siberia of Jiangsu. Here I built a hut and farmed for nine years. During my spare time I drank and talked with old friends of mine who'd also been sent there. We talked about current affairs, about our experiences and about the Marxist texts we'd read, trying to analyse our own and our country's experience. As far as I'm concerned, those nine years weren't entirely wasted; I had the chance to think a lot. We believed that the "gang of four" would one day fall from power, but it was difficult to say when. Would it be in our lifetime?

That day finally came and the "gang of four" was smashed. Like everyone else in the country I was excited beyond words. After a three-day drinking spree with friends, I went and hunted for my fountain pen. I had to write; the urge to do so had to find an outlet. But I hadn't written anything for thirteen years, I'd forgotten a lot of words and couldn't even remember how to write. Like an invalid who'd been bedridden for thirteen years, I made my way along by clinging to the walls. I started by writing a few practice essays and playscripts to gradually reactivate distant memories, and then I put my energies into writing a short story. The former editors of the revived *People's Literature* were hunting everywhere for old writers, and when they located me I had already finished a story called *Dedication*. This was later published in the magazine and won a 1980 best short story award.

My family returned to Suzhou from the coast, and at fifty I became a professional writer again. It had taken me twenty-five years and three rises and two falls to fully enter this unenviable profession.

Strictly speaking, fifty was the age at which I really began to write; the preceding twenty-five were just a rehearsal and a tempering period. In the eight years since the "gang of four's" downfall I've published numerous novellas and short stories, won four awards and been elected a Jiangsu provincial people's deputy. I've also been given the title of "model worker" by Suzhou municipality. At the fourth congress of the Chinese Writers' Association, I was elected a vice-chairman of the association. All this has made me extremely happy, happy because Chinese intellectuals have finally emerged from their suffering and are starting to receive attention and trust. Whenever I travel to Beijing to receive an award, I always feel sad that so many of my friends aren't there. Some lost their lives, others their talents during those painful years. Because of this, I always feel I have a historic responsibility, a duty to write about all kinds of human life and social events, to pour out my blood and tears, burn them to emit a weak light, so that people who are moving towards happiness through that dark night will be consoled when they see it in the distance, and feel that they will soon reach their destination.

March 3, 1985

Translated by Yu Fanqin

Deep Within a Lane

SUZHOU, that ancient city, is sleeping soundly. She is lying peacefully within the embrace of waters, like a water-lily on a silver riverbed. Dimly-lit streetlamps illuminate white poplars in the autumn wind, casting dancing tree shadows on to the stone roads and lending the streets a hazy, sleepy air.

In the northeast corner of the city, in a deeply receding small lane paved with stone flags, a light still shone in one window. Under the light sat a young woman at a desk, her hands cupping her chin, rapt in silent thought.

She had a high-bridged nose and a slightly protruding forehead by no means too large and well in proportion to the bridge of her nose. Her eyes were gleaming dark pools and her long, sparse lashes could almost be counted in the lamplight. Two braids hung down each side of her face and were caught up again at the back of her neck into one braid extending down to her waist, with a flowered scarf knotted carelessly at the point where the two braids became one. Ah! Why were there such dark shadows under her eyes? It did not look as if she had been crying, nor did it seem to be for lack of sleep; rather it appeared to be a mark left by pain and suffering.

Very few people in this lane knew what this young woman did. Her neighbours only knew that she was not at home during the day and studied late into the night. Only the postman knew her name was Xu Wenxia and that she was a worker in a cotton mill, because he often delivered to her beautifully-written envelopes. These she frowned at and even tore into tiny pieces in front of him.

Xu Wenxia put down her hands and opened the algebra book on her desk. Yet she read nothing, overwhelmed by a feeling of wretchedness. Such wretchedness, typical to young girls, had often swept through her recently. Whenever it did so it brought in its wake both fear and resentment and caused memories of shame, mortification and tears to rise once again before her eyes. . . .

It was a damp autumnal dusk on what was essentially a bitterly cold winter's night. A group of coquettish-looking women were loitering on the streets, at the corners of houses and in the entrance-ways of alleys close to the hotels outside Changmen. Some moved like ghosts; others leaned like drunkards against the telegraph poles, cigarettes dangling from their lips, their arms crossed below their breasts, deliberately pushing them upwards. Their eyes were all fixed on the entrances to the hotels and the passers-by, and every time a man walked past a clamour would erupt:

"Come home with me!"

"Shameless tarts! Disgusting creatures!" A passer-by hurled abuse at them.

Such abuse immediately aroused a loud wave of uncaring laughter: "Stupid idiot! Pig! Bastard!" A stream of invective poured out from the women. Xu Wenxia was one of those women. At that time she was called Fourth Sister by the Madam. She was only a child of seventeen and her gaunt, thickly-powdered face looked even paler under the streetlights. . . .

All this was long past and seemed to belong to another world, but still whenever Xu Wenxia remembered it she used to shudder.

In 1952 the People's Government brought all prostitutes in to training institutes where they were cured of disease, given the opportunity to talk about their hardships and trained in productive skills. Xu Wenxia spent the most unforgettable year of her life there. She did not know what her mother was like, nor how a mother's love felt, but she felt there could be no greater happiness than this, for life's greatest happiness is to be able to lift up one's head in the sunlight and be a real person.

When that year was over Xu Wenxia began working at the New Life Yarn-Dyeing Factory. Later she was moved to the Dasheng Cloth Factory, where she operated a loom, and finally went to work at the Qinda Cotton Mill. On seeing her youth and intelligent face the mill's head said to her, "Don't do weaving. Go to the electricians' shop; we need skilful hands there."

Life became bright for Xu Wenxia as respect, honour and tender care all came her way. She entered an astonishing world, for never before had she known the dignity of being a human being.

Yet, slowly, Xu Wenxia became worried and scared, scared of the special, burning glances young men gave her, scared lest such glances pierce her heart and discover the evil spectre behind her, for when that happened those special looks would turn into disdain and the fire would become ice. She buried her past deeply, and fortunately no one knew of it after she had changed her job several times. Let it pass, let it disperse like a nightmare.

And yet, what about love and the joy a family brings? Xu Wenxia dared not think of this and was afraid when others mentioned it, frightened lest someone bring up the hardships of life before Liberation and afraid most of all when her women friends prepared their trousseaux. Gradually she became more solitary, and in the quiet of the night she would weep into her quilt. She kept to herself as much as possible. And so she lived in this old, small lane. No one disturbed her here, only occasionally would someone pass by, their leather shoes giving off a hollow sound as they hit the stone flags. She put all her energy into studying, passing the long nights in the company of books, forgetting everything. The young men were not willing to give up on her and often wrote letters which filled Xu Wenxia with sadness until finally she began tearing them up without looking at them. "Who could feel real love for a woman who has been a prostitute? Keep away — it's bitter medicine!"

Her misery made Xu Wenxia restless. She stood up from the desk and walked around the room before forcing herself to sit down once more, cupping her head in her hands, her fingers pressing against her throbbing temples as if she were trying to force out all her random thoughts. She inhaled deeply:

"Give me work and let others have love!"

She opened her algebra book once again and put all her effort into exploring the secrets of equations. After some time the letters danced and wavered before her eyes. She rubbed them, hoping to recall her concentration, but in a short time they were moving again, like ripples on a lake. . . .

Could it be that it was too hot? She pushed open the window; there was a slight breeze outside and the leaves rustled. The night air and the sound of autumn can make one sleepy, but Xu Wenxia simply felt even more miserable. She knew why she was miserable. The image of the technician Zhang Jun, a university graduate, continued to haunt her: his square, youthful and ruddy face, his constant smile as they talked together, how he raced over to see her as if looking for something and then, face flushed, left again without a word. Xu Wenxia knew why she was upset by this but was consciously unwilling to admit it, for it was in just such a way that she had beaten back many onslaughts of love. What was happening to her today? She had said that she would not think of it, but she was doing so nonetheless. "Why did he come here today, first knocking lightly on the door, waiting and then knocking again as if he wanted to come in but didn't dare? Why was his face so red? Don't look so red, comrade, as if someone like me could make fun of anyone else. Ah! Why didn't he say anything? He's quite a good talker but today he was stuttering. Turning the pages of my books with great concentration! As if he hadn't read them all already. He wants to help me study algebra and to teach me physics! What a mess! I've already agreed, so what can I do if he's got some other idea in his head?"

Xu Wenxia's quiet heart had been disturbed, all her lines of defence had crumbled; she had ignored many meaningful glances and torn up many enticing letters, but she had no way of avoiding Zhang Jun's pure, innocent eyes. She could not stop her thoughts racing wildly, at one moment feeling full of happiness, so happy that her heart felt like bursting! The next moment she was full of fear, so frightened it was as if she had leapt into a bottomless pit. She felt stifled by her various contradictory feelings and anguish, and the tragic events of her past resurfaced. She leaned on the desk and sobbed, her shoulders shaking under the soft lamplight.

Outside it began to rain and water dripped from the eaves on to the stone flags below in a continuous chattering flow. . . .

As autumn turned to winter Xu Wenxia's heart began to blossom like a spring flower.

As soon as work was over Zhang Jun came over to Xu Wenxia's home and sat opposite her, silently watching her, looking at her blushing face.

"Come on, let's not waste time."

Zhang Jun laughed and opened the textbook. There was no better teacher in the world, for not only did he talk but also acted out things, somehow finding many apposite and exciting examples to use in explanation. Zhang Jun did not realize that his wisdom was like an endlessly flowing river once in the presence of Xu Wenxia.

When Xu Wenxia prepared her homework Zhang Jun would sit at another table and do his own assignments. At these times the room was quite silent, with only the scratching sounds of pens against paper. Zhang Jun was able to sit at a desk immobile for two to three hours at a stretch, but Xu Wenxia was concerned lest he overwork, so she came over and tweaked his ears and scratched his back. Zhang Jun shouted, "You're disturbing my work!"

Xu Wenxia giggled and sat down again. Not long afterwards she pushed an apple towards him. Zhang Jun put the apple on the table, not touching it at first, but in a while he picked it up to look at it and then went over to feel in Xu Wenxia's pockets for a pen-knife.

"Now it's you who's disturbing me!"

"You gave me the apple!"

After this interlude neither was able to continue studying, so they tidied away their books and began talking about everything under the sun. Zhang Jun loved talking about the future: he was always five years ahead. "I'll be an engineer then and you'll be a technician."

"Do you think I can be a technician?"

"Only if you don't misbehave when you're studying," said Zhang Jun, tapping Xu Wenxia on the forehead. "We'll be working together then and if a machine goes wrong we'll mend it together. My face will be covered in oil and you won't be able to recognize me!"

"Even if you fell into a vat of dye I'd still be able to recognize you."

"Just think how good it would be if there were such a couple in the world, working together, going home together, going out with their children on a Sunday."

Xu Wenxia's heart began to thud at these words and her face flushed. "What's the point in talking about someone else's affairs?"

The more Zhang Jun talked, the further he ranged and the more attractive it sounded. Xu Wenxia felt as if she were steeping in a vat of warm water. It was the first time she had felt the happiness and excitement love brings.

When there was nothing more to say they would go for a stroll, arm in arm. Even though the evening air was refreshing in the streets of Suzhou, people were few and far between and the sound of a *wonton*-seller's clappers nearby somehow made the silence of the streets even more profound. They tended to go to places where others did not, treading on the fallen leaves of plane trees, strangely comforted by the rustling sound they made. Xu Wenxia loved to kick at the brittle leaves, sending them off in all directions. They never knew how far they walked, but they always turned back when they saw the towering dark shadow of Beisi Pagoda.

Zhang Jun came to Xu Wenxia's place every day. When he was really busy he would come before he went to bed and say to her, "Sleep well, Wenxia. I'll see you tomorrow."

Xu Wenxia was used to waiting until 10.30 for Zhang Jun, and if he did not come by then she would go to bed. Then she would hear the key turn and Zhang Jun's large hand would pat her quilt a couple of times. "Sleep well, Wenxia..." he would say. And only then could she really sleep soundly.

Xu Wenxia had already given up all hope in the ocean of love but suddenly she had come across a lifebelt and grasped it desperately, deeply afraid lest she lose it. At night she often dreamed of Zhang Jun pointing at her and cursing sternly, "I thought you were pure, untainted, but in fact you were a prostitute, a shameless creature. I don't want anything more to do with you!" Xu Wenxia wept and held on to Zhang

Jun. "Don't blame me, I was forced by the old society...." He ignored her, pulled his hand away and left. Xu Wenxia threw herself on him only to find there was no one there. She awoke to find herself in bed in a cold sweat, her tears soaking the pillow as she continued sobbing.

Xu Wenxia could not sleep again as so much anguish came to torment her:

"What can I do? Will it really be like that? Suppose Zhang Jun discovers? I should tell him . . . no, he wouldn't be able to forgive me. A man like him could be loved by any number of pure young girls, so why would he want someone who's been a prostitute? I can't tell him, I can't!" Xu Wenxia pulled her top closely around her and turned on the bedside lamp — she was terrified and she felt sad. She could not lose Zhang Jun; she could not do without his love.

One bright morning in early winter the weather was unusually warm. On their day off the people of Suzhou went wandering in the ancient gardens.

Xu Wenxia was wearing a cream silk padded jacket shot through with white flowers. The jacket was rather tight but it made her seem even more slim and attractive. Hanging below her jacket her braids seemed even longer, making her look tall and elegant. She carried a yellow straw handbag in her left hand and her right hand was through Zhang Jun's arm. They walked silently into Liu Garden, strolling along quiet, twisting paths. Their footsteps matched each other's, light and brisk, their hard leather soles sounding rhythmically against the cobblestones, almost like notes being plucked on a *pipa*. Piled up on either side of the path were strangely-shaped mock mountains of pointed stalagmites and towering, irregular and pitted narrow rocks from Lake Tai; late-flowering chrysanthemums, still vigorous, peeked through holes in the rocks. Xu Wenxia's eyes were brimming like jet-black drops of oil in clear water, carefree and full of joy. "Ah! If only it could always be like this!"

They stood for a moment by a limpid rock pool beside some children calling to the brightly coloured goldfish and then they turned and went back past the towering stone peaks until they came across a small building.

"Let's go up into that building!" Xu Wenxia gestured towards it with her right hand.

Zhang Jun pulled her by the hand up an artificial hill.

"Hey! I said the building!" Xu Wenxia stumbled as she raced up the hill. "I told you to go up into the building but you climb this hill instead!"

"Don't complain — we've already gone up the building!"

Xu Wenxia looked — yes, they had indeed climbed up into the building after all, for the artificial hill constituted the building's steps, so that people climbed effortlessly to the building as they enjoyed the mountain scene. Xu Wenxia could not help laughing but then she stopped and sighed, "How clever the builders of these gardens must have been, Jun, putting all their efforts into making life more beautiful."

"Come on, let's go. What's the point of saying something like that?"

As they went along the twisting corridor Xu Wenxia felt rather distressed. "Ah, well, it might seem pointless, but if you understood the trouble the builder of this garden went to you would sympathize with him, forgive his mistakes and help him achieve his hopes."

Zhang Jun was dumbfounded when he saw the distressed look in Xu Wenxia's eyes. "What is it, Wenxia? Is something bothering you?"

"No, it's nothing."

"Then why aren't you happy?"

"I am happy. I'm always happy when I'm with you." Xu Wenxia forced a smile. "Let's go. What's that up ahead?"

Ahead there was a full-moon shaped entrance-way through which could be seen a rural scene, with bean trellises, gourd trellises and fragrant, freshly-turned black earth. They walked beneath a wistaria trellis from which gourds hung down, decorating the dried vines suspended above their heads like a myriad stars.

Zhang Jun was silent for a while and then said hesitantly, "Wenxia, tell me truly what you think of me."

"What can I say. . . ? I don't think I'd ever . . . find anyone like you again."

Zhang Jun leaped up, his face as bright as when the sun breaks through the clouds and shines everywhere. "Wenxia! Let's get married!"

Xu Wenxia felt a sudden jolt as mingled joy and fear assaulted her. She went white and her lips trembled. It was a long time before she said, "Let's go on."

Zhang Jun's high spirits plummeted, transforming into a faraway, murmuring stream.

"Wenxia, the road of life is both short and long. Two people can walk together hand in hand along this road, sharing the same ideals. When one becomes tired the other can support her; when one is successful the other can congratulate him. Just think, there would be no mountain we couldn't climb, no river we couldn't cross!"

Xu Wenxia was moved almost to tears. If there could be someone like him to go through life beside her it would be like a dream, a beautiful picture! However, she could not help regarding him in doubt, asking him silently, "Would you still say this if you knew?" She lowered her head in anguish and said, "Let's go."

An earth mound appeared ahead, its top full of maple trees, their leaves dyed the red of sunrise by an early frost. Halfway up the mound on a stone bench a man was sitting, his back facing Xu Wenxia and the collar of his overcoat raised as he sat in the sun. The sound of Xu Wenxia's shoes attracted his attention and he turned to reveal a flat-looking face, like skin tightly stretched over a drum, on which his eyes, nose and mouth made little impression. Like two slits in the drum-skin his sharp eyes were riveted on Xu Wenxia. Waiting until Xu Wenxia had come up right before him he suddenly stood up and said respectfully, "How are you, Fourth Sister? Are you still living in Suzhou?"

"You! You've . . . so you've come here too. Goodbye. Jun, let's go to the top of the hill to take a look."

Pulling Zhang Jun's hand Xu Wenxia sped up to the top of the hill. She was deeply disturbed — breathing hard, her eyes blinking rapidly, her stomach fluttering and shivering all over.

Zhang Jun looked back at the man and saw that he was already lazily making his way down the hill.

"Who was that and why did he call you 'Fourth Sister'?"

"No one special, just someone I once knew. 'Fourth Sister' is my childhood name." Xu Wenxia shivered. After a moment she said, "Let's go back. It's cold here and there's nothing much to see."

Zhang Jun noted how strange Xu Wenxia looked and felt ill-at-ease as if something had been left unresolved, but nevertheless went reluctantly through the garden gate.

A soft knock came at the door. A pause, followed by another soft knock. Xu Wenxia's face transformed from surprise to joy and she sprang up from the bed. "It's him! He forgot his key again!"

She opened the door softly and slowly, hoping to rush out and surprise Zhang Jun.

Suddenly a flat face floated before her eyes, startling her and causing a cold wave to sweep all over her. It was Zhu Guohun! Zhu Guohun, whom they had encountered the other day in the garden. Xu Wenxia went rigid with shock, her hand against the side of the door, not knowing whether to close it or to let him in. Smiling slightly, Zhu Guohun looked up and down the lane and then, without waiting for an invitation, swiftly stepped inside, bowed and greeted her as "Miss Xu". When she heard him call her "Miss Xu" rather than "Fourth Sister" Xu Wenxia felt even more unsettled. "The devil! He knows everything!" She strove to appear calm and not reveal the slightest hint of discomfort.

"How have you been doing all these years, Manager Zhu?"

"Hee hee, nothing much. I did some unlawful business a few years ago and was given a little education by the government, doing reform through labour for a couple of years. This government is very different from the old one and you don't get beaten or cursed when you're punished. Labour . . . everyone works hard. Well, Miss Xu, I hear you've been getting on in the world the past two years!" Zhu Guohun was attempting to learn a new way of speaking but a few old-style expressions slipped in when he was careless. "Getting on. . . ."

"People don't talk about 'getting on' anymore." Xu Wenxia felt a wave of revulsion.

"Indeed, indeed. Labour is glorious." Zhu Guohun was measuring up the room, looking at everything, hoping to discover the owner's secrets from her every object.

Xu Wenxia was on the alert, her heart beating furiously, not knowing what his next step would be.

Zhu Guohun's gaze returned from the objects to Xu Wenxia's face, his own taking on a confident and careless expression.

Xu Wenxia kept her gaze fixed on his flat face, her expression revealing a mixture of ashamed cowardice and burning anger. This profiteer had been the first to possess her before Liberation, treating her body cruelly and destructively. What did he want now? He said nothing, simply stretching out his neck and breathing in and out through his round, round lips. Xu Wenxia fell back, feeling nauseated and seriously considering slapping his flat thing of a face. But she restrained herself. Ever since she had bumped into him she had been scared of this man, feeling as if she had somehow given him a handle over her.

Zhu Guohun began speaking casually. "Hah! Hah! You've got your head screwed on right. Fourth Sister, hooking someone like Zhang Jun, a university student, a very clever fellow, oh yes, very promising! Be careful though, you should be more careful about hiding what happened in the past or it could backfire on you!" Zhu Guohun blinked his small eyes and deliberately spoke more slowly. "Of course, I'm no blabbermouth and I certainly wouldn't reveal our relationship before Liberation. After all, a gentleman will always help others achieve their aims, isn't that so?"

Xu Wenxia felt as if she had been hit by lightning; her hands and feet went cold and the calm she had fought to sustain dissolved as she asked him the question that preoccupied her, "How do you know so much?"

"Hee hee! I'm a businessman and it's my trade to know about other people's business."

Xu Wenxia went extremely pale as a multitude of thoughts swiftly churned inside her: should she curse him roundly, throw him out or go to the police? They were all easy to do. And yet . . . what if Zhang Jun were to know, what if this bully told Zhang Jun everything and twisted it all. . . ? She dared not think about it. She felt increasingly dizzy and his flat face seemed to stretch infinitely before her eyes, becoming larger and taking on a terrifying aspect. Xu Wenxia blinked, her heart turbulent.

"What is it you want? We understand each other, Manager Zhu, so lay your cards on the table and come out with it."

"Oh, I don't want anything — after all, this isn't before Liberation. However, I've got myself a small stall now and I'm a bit short of capital. I was hoping to borrow some from you. We all know how things stand — everyone has their bad moments."

Xu Wenxia gritted her teeth and felt she would explode with anger, but she dared say nothing and instead almost automatically stretched out a trembling hand to place a pile of notes on the table.

Zhu Guohun lifted himself up and said thank you. He placed his thumb on his lips, wet it with saliva and counted the money in a practised manner. Then with a laugh he put it back on the table.

"Miss Xu, it's not that I'm complaining that you've given me too little, nor will I mention how much I spent on you in the past, but really, this twenty yuan cannot be put to good use. If you don't have any more on you at the moment I'll come back to visit you tomorrow!"

Xu Wenxia bit her lip and her face became suffused with anger, but she pulled open a drawer and flung down one month's wages before turning to fall on the bed, burying her head and weeping bitterly.

Gradually winter assumed a bitterly cold face, with a northwest wind blowing day after day and snowflakes fluttering down.

Xu Wenxia sat in a daze by the window, her face thinner, her gaze blank, staring fixedly through the glass, watching snowflakes hitting the window, changing into drops of water and flowing down like tears. The snow beyond the window increased, as larger flakes came flying down and covering the world in a sheet of white.

The alarm clock at the head of the bed ticked unhurriedly. Xu Wenxia looked at it again. "Why hasn't he come yet?"

"I know — Zhu Guohun has told him!" It was as if Xu Wenxia's heart was hanging from cobwebs, dropping down swiftly and dangling in mid-air. "He's angry! No, he's upset because his beloved used to be a prostitute!"

"Dringg. . . ." The alarm suddenly went off. The sound startled her and she swiftly went over to stop it before sitting down listlessly on the bed, her hand against her heart to restrain its beating. When Zhang Jun was not beside her she was afraid of every sound, scared lest Zhu Guohun once more enmesh her. She really wanted to leave this cold, silent room, but perhaps it would prove to be her haven.

"No, he doesn't know yet. Zhu Guohun wouldn't let go of me so easily — a snake like him would suck me dry and then eat me up!"

Zhang Jun came in, stamped his feet and shook off the snow on his raincoat. His face was red with the cold, and frosty breath issued from his mouth.

"It's really snowing hard out there — you should go out and take a look. There hasn't been snow like this in years."

Xu Wenxia flew over to him and held him. "Why did you take so long? Why are you always so late these days?"

"That's just your imagination — it's exactly the same as before. Don't worry unnecessarily, Wenxia; whatever happens I won't ever leave you."

Xu Wenxia held him even tighter. "Don't leave me, don't get rid of me! No, even if you did, I wouldn't hold it against you."

Zhang Jun released himself from her grasp, took her hand and looked at her in surprise. "You've got thinner and there are tears in your eyes. You're upset about something but you're hiding it. You aren't willing to tell me and I'm not allowed to ask. Ah, dearest girl, whatever have you done that I could not forgive you?" Zhang Jun's lips trembled. He wanted to say something but restrained himself, finally reiterating the words he said so often, "Let's get married, Wenxia."

Xu Wenxia released Zhang Jun's hand and retreated. "Leave me, Zhang Jun. I'm not worthy of you, you'll regret it, so leave me!" As she said this she threw herself on to him once more and, buried in his embrace, wiped her tears.

Zhang Jun stroked her hair, both pitying and anxious. "Don't be upset. You mustn't think I'm only playing around." He patted her. "There's another meeting I have to go to. You go over your work and then I'll teach you something new tomorrow. Don't worry so much!"

Xu Wenxia reverted to her trance-like state. "He's gone again! He's always in such a hurry these days. Okay, then, the end's in sight, it's here, it was bound to happen one day, so the sooner the better!" How could she study her algebra? Instead, almost unconsciously, she went to open a clothes-chest, put on her new overcoat and new shoes, tied on her red scarf and turned slowly before the mirror, a slight smile on her lips and teardrops in her eyes. She sighed, took them off item by item, took out some patterned fabrics and silk, looked at them and then replaced them. Her trousseau. She did not believe it herself, but these things had been bought in preparation for marriage. She had dreamed of that day, not daring to believe it could ever come, yet still she had gone ahead and bought all those things. Recently, when Zhang Jun had not been around, she went through them, admiring them, dreaming beautiful dreams of a dazzling vision of life. She liked to think and imagine, particularly at times of sorrow and disappointment.

"How are you, Miss Xu? Oh, I see you're getting ready for your wedding — I'll beg a celebratory drink from you." It was Zhu Guohun. When Zhang Jun left just now he forgot to lock the door.

As soon as Xu Wenxia saw this man her dreams shattered. She slammed the clothes-chest shut and glared at him. "What have you come for this time?"

"Last time . . . I borrowed a bit of money from you . . . and, well, I'm broke again."

"And I'm supposed to be your debtor? Get out!" Xu Wenxia stood up straight, her eyes red, itching to ignite into flames and burn this man to ashes.

"What's the point in getting so angry, Miss Xu? No one should keep everything for themselves or they'll get spoiled — no, life's benefits should be shared."

"You!" Xu Wenxia cried out, the flames of anger hot within her. All her happiness and joy had been smashed by him, she should fight against him! But then, when she turned and looked at the clothes-chest her resolution weakened again and with a shaking hand she took out twenty yuan.

Zhu Guohun had not thought it would be so easy to extort money from her the second time. This made him look at Xu Wenxia and discover how slim yet well-rounded she had become in the last few years. High-breasted with rounded arms, she exuded youthful attractiveness. His heart beating, an evil thought took shape. His face became suffused with a flush: "I'll sleep here tonight."

"Thwack! Thwack!" Two clear slaps rang out. Zhu Guohun had not been able to forestall them and leapt back, rubbing his cheeks. "Hey! Hey! What are you so moralistic about? After all, it won't be the first time."

Xu Wenxia flung herself forward furiously, like an angry lion, all her anguish, shame and anger uniting together as she pounded at Zhu Guohun with all her strength.

Zhu Guohun was by no means badly hurt but he cried out in a small voice, "You're persecuting me!"

Xu Wenxia was totally uncaring and bit hard on Zhu Guohun's arm.

Zhu Guohun shot up in genuine pain and shoved her aside. He picked up a stool but reconsidered and gently put it down again. "Don't be stupid. Think of your future."

Xu Wenxia acted as if she had not heard, seized the stool and flung it at him with all her strength. Zhu Guohun, realizing things were not going well, turned and slipped out of the door as the stool hit the wall with a crash.

Xu Wenxia stood outside the entrance to Zhang Jun's dormitory, her hair dishevelled, her face pale. She had a determined light in her eyes. "Go on! Tell him! Bring shame upon yourself, make yourself unhappy and alone!" Although she thought all this her feet were unwilling to move, as if there were a deep abyss before the threshold from which she could not be rescued if she stepped into it.

Zhang Jun finished washing and picked up the bowl full of soapy water. He was going tc throw the water out of the door when he noticed there was someone out there and swiftly retracted it, pouring half the bowlful over himself in the process.

"Wenxia!" Zhang Jun was startled, but when he saw how she looked he was even more astonished and pulled her by the hand to sit on the edge of the bed. "What's happened, Wenxia? Tell me quickly!"

Xu Wenxia seemed to have lost her reason and stared at Zhang Jun blankly.

"What is it, Wenxia?" Zhang Jun shook her by the arm. "Tell me quickly. You make me worried when I see you look like this."

Xu Wenxia still looked blank but then she suddenly turned and threw herself into his arms, her tears like a river breaking through a dyke.

Zhang Jun was even more upset. "Don't cry. If you have something to say, say it quickly, don't cry! It's not good to let others hear you."

Xu Wenxia cried without cease, letting her tears tell the history of her life, her anguish and her shame. She cried non-stop for over ten minutes until she felt that the object blocking her heart had been washed away and then, slowly, she quietened down, sighed deeply and frankly told Zhang Jun the story of her past.

How many nights had she buried these words deep within her breast? Then every sentence had cut into her breast like a sharp knife gouging her. And yet, now, as she revealed everything, she was not at all afraid.

When she began she still felt some embarrassment and spoke disjointedly, but gradually she began talking with increasing fluency and indignation, and by the end she felt she had grown stronger and greater, as if she were standing on stage, denouncing the grief and indignation she had experienced because of the old society.

When Xu Wenxia had finished speaking she took Zhang Jun's large, long hand. When she saw his stunned expression she knew that they would have to part and was unable to restrain her tears.

Zhang Jun had been deeply angered by Xu Wenxia's account. It was as if he had heard a disturbing story. He leapt up angrily from the bed, "Where is that bastard? It's outrageous that anyone should dare to do anything like that nowadays! I'm going to look for him."

"Don't go. Let the police handle it. Don't be upset because of me. I feel I should apologize to you since you gave me your heart and I tricked you for so long. Forgive me, Zhang Jun, I was afraid of winter's cold and always hoped spring would last forever. . . ."

"Don't cry, Wenxia, how can I blame you?"

"No, you should. I was much too selfish. Why did I want to hang on to you and make you share my shame and pain? Leave me, Zhang Jun, I beg you, and while perhaps at first you won't be used to it, you'll forget in time. You shouldn't forget entirely. Please remember always someone who, although she couldn't go forward with you hand in hand, will always bless you. . . ." Xu Wenxia could not continue and slumped down, weeping again.

Zhang Jun felt extremely upset. His heart was being pulled violently in two, by the sobs behind him and by the night sky outside. It was on just such a night, outside Changmen, beside a hotel, under the streetlights at dusk. . . .

Zhang Jun was silent, deep in thought, which calmed Xu Wenxia, for this was the best ending she could have envisaged, everything ending in thoughtful silence. She hauled herself up and silently, yet filled with emotion, cried out in her heart, "Goodbye!" And lightly, silently, backed out. . . .

It was late and the air was almost freezing. A half-moon hung above the eaves and thick frost silently covered the roofs.

Zhang Jun paced back and forth in the deeply receding cobbled lane, looking at Xu Wenxia's far-off lighted window and turning back every time he reached it. "What can I say? What can I say to her?" He thought of the young woman beneath the lamp, a young woman who was the embodiment of beauty and goodness, with whom it was impossible to link the word "prostitute". But she *was* linked! Zhang Jun demanded thunderously: Who put the blemish on the pure white silk? Who spat into the clear stream? It was impossible to blame her, for how could a weak orphan manage to survive in those dark times?

If this were the misfortune of an ordinary girl Zhang Jun undoubtedly would be able to sympathize and immediately understand. But this was Xu Wenxia, the woman beside whom he wanted to spend the rest of his life. . . . He hesitated, walking back and forth in the lane. Many past events rose before his eyes — he thought of the days full of joy and excitement he had spent with Xu Wenxia. Then the sky had seemed bluer, the road less rough, and sadness had been but the prelude to joy while defeats were the symbols of success. All had been filled with life's force, hope and faith. All this had been inspired by a young woman, a young woman who had struggled out of a cruel sea and offered him a pure heart. She had endured so much pain in loving him and had yearned so much for a beautiful life and constant self-improvement. Slowly Zhang Jun felt he was diminished and insignificant, a hunched-up coward, the defeated soldier of customs and tradition.

He raised his head and asked the pure night sky, "What disgrace is there in being with a woman such as she? Why don't you dare say, 'I do not ever want to leave you. We will go forward hand in hand on the road of life'? Why don't you dare say it? What's wrong in saying it?" Unconsciously Zhang Jun cried out loud, then he turned round swiftly and raced to Xu Wenxia's door only to discover he had forgotten his key again. He banged his fist hard against the door. . . .

Suzhou, that ancient, beautiful city, was sleeping soundly now. Only from the deep recesses of a small lane came the sound of knocking.

October 1955

Translated by Ralph Lake

Tang Qiaodi

THERE are many elderly female workers in the Tailong Cotton Mill who have the syllable "*di*", an ancient term for the wife of a younger brother, in their names, names like Qiaodi, Jindi, Fudi, Gendi, Mingdi, Zhaodi and Laidi. When choices in good first syllables ran out some just ended up being called Adi. The original meaning of the word *di* no longer applies and it was instead employed by a practitioner of glyphomancy claiming to be able to influence the fortunes of others through the manipulation of the different components of Chinese characters. *Di*, composed of the character "female" next to that representing a younger brother, has strong implications of male superiority. When your child is quite obviously female but you wanted a male and cannot get her to be one, all you can do is place the character for female to the left of "brother". With names like Zhaodi and Laidi the aim is even more apparent — next time you will not bear another daughter because you have called for (*zhao*) a little brother (*di*) or will let a little brother come (*laidi*).

These women with *di* in their names did not come from distinguished families, nor were they born into the literati. Instead their fates were all sad ones, for they came into a world of poverty and hardship and, silently, went into the next world still in poverty and hardship.

Some of them came to work in the Cotton Mill as "foreign mill lassies" or what are now referred to as female textile workers. As far as their work is concerned the "foreign mill lassies" and female textile workers do exactly the same job but there is a world of difference in their status. I used to live in a dilapidated wooden house opposite the Tailong Cotton Mill and knew how "foreign mill lassies" were treated:

Whenever the market price of cotton was expected to rise suddenly every spindle had to be put to work and Tailong Cotton Mill used to put up a sign advertising for workers. Then women with *di* in their names and without connections or the wherewithal to buy presents would come crowding in from the surrounding countryside to stand before the Mill's gates. Those awaiting work would arrive quietly in the small hours and some squatted, some stood, some coughed and some sighed. There were also some who cried; perhaps they were newly-widowed or had run away after quarrelling with their mother-in-law. As the sky began to brighten they started getting restless, the atmosphere becoming increasingly tense as the sky grew lighter, with shouting, weeping, cursing, pushing, moving bricks around and crowding tightly together before the iron gates of the Mill. Some stood on bricks, some on others' toes, trying to think of any method at all to make themselves taller because the Mill would not take short workers who found it hard to reach the raw yarn at the top of the machines.

When the sun finally climbed as far as my small wooden building the iron gates of the Mill were pulled open to a roar of shouting . . . and then a sudden silence fell, and no one dared move. The Mill was heavily guarded from within by men armed with staves or hoses ready to thrash anyone daring to rush in. Finally someone who looked like an overseer would look around and drag in a few tall ones with good bodies and pretty faces, one by one.

Tang Qiaodi was very tall and by no means ugly, so she went to work in the Mill as a child of fourteen and was twenty-three in 1949, the year China was liberated. Thus, while you could say she was still young, she was in fact already a mature worker with ten years' experience under her belt.

I am the same age as Tang Qiaodi. After graduating from a secondary teachers' school I was sent to work as a night-school teacher at Tailong Cotton Mill. Although I was new as a teacher there, when I had lived opposite the Mill the women working there used to shelter from the rain in my home or leave things there that they could not take into the Mill, including children. So I was quite familiar with many of those called *di* and we would smile and nod on meeting each other. Naturally this included Tang Qiaodi.

Although Tang Qiaodi had been working since childhood she was not afraid of speaking in public. She had a hoarse voice and spoke in a well-organized and lively manner. In the early years of the People's Republic there were numerous political campaigns in which the oral description of past suffering played a major role. Tang Qiaodi used to represent other old workers by speaking in public about their past hardships, reducing both those beside her on the platform and those in the audience to tears. I also wept when I heard her — those women with *di* in their names had gone from poverty and hardship into hell! Moved, I went to find

Tang Qiaodi for more in-depth information and wrote a long report for a newspaper. It did not occur to me that because of this Tang Qiaodi would become a symbol, wanted everywhere to give speeches and attend meetings; because of this too I was given titles such as cultural and educational committee member, sports committee member and special reporter.

The newspaper office told me there was a need for more articles on such symbols, describing not only their hardship but also covering more positive aspects such as how they went through the process of liberation and threw themselves into the production struggle as mistresses of their own fate. I took note of this and kept a close eye on Tang Qiaodi's every action, often seeking her out for a talk or participating in her small group meetings.

Tang Qiaodi certainly had an extraordinary capacity for hard work. She was young, strong and skilful, constantly increased her production output, formed small advanced groups of workers and initiated work competitions, all with great enthusiasm and zeal. Whatever she did I wrote about and was able to publish every piece. Some people said I made a fast buck off Tang Qiaodi's back, but in fact that was an injustice, because the money was barely enough to buy some peanuts, and what is more, most of them were eaten by other people. It was not money of which I had been thinking, but of the time before Liberation when I used to lie reading in my small wooden building while Tang Qiaodi and the others were sweating blood day in day out. So now I wanted to do whatever I could to help the liberation of the working class.

Tang Qiaodi often came looking for me too. She

could not read or write and often wanted me to write a reply for her to a primary schoolchild's letter or help her compose group pledges or conditions for competitions. It was no fault of hers that she was illiterate — it was the result of the old, bad days. And so, no matter how busy I was, I always immediately helped her out, urging her as I did so, "You should come along to the evening classes, Qiaodi. Workers are standing up now and must have education; so if you come to the classes I promise to teach you to the best of my ability. It will take someone as intelligent as you less than two years!"

"Truly?"

"Truly!"

"Good! I'll come for sure!"

And Tang Qiaodi did indeed come, bringing with her a new notebook and a new fountain pen, and sat, very well-behaved, in the last row. When I saw her I was extremely pleased and taught with greater enthusiasm, projecting every word clearly and distinctly towards Tang Qiaodi.

Yet, only a few days later, when Tang Qiaodi sat down in the classroom she yawned and eventually put her head down on the desk and slept, needing to be shaken awake by someone at the end of class.

I kept Tang Qiaodi behind and asked if I had been teaching badly, whether she had not understood something or was not interested in a particular topic.

Vaguely Tang Qiaodi replied, "No, I just wanted to sleep. . . ."

"But that's no good! You should remember that not only did the exploiting classes squeeze you dry but they also deprived you of your right to an education. A deprivation of this nature is extremely serious because it causes ignorance amongst the working class and thus hinders you from ever becoming completely emancipated! You should think of. . . ."

"I don't have the strength to think. I'm too tired."

I was absolutely stunned! It was true that ever since Tang Qiaodi had increased her productive output she had been walking back and forth non-stop while working, covering over thirty *li* in one day's shift. And that was not like walking in the countryside, where all you need to do is to swing your arms and go forward in the fresh air, with the blue sky and white clouds above and perhaps, if you are lucky, the sound of birdsong, the fragrance of flowers and a murmuring stream. Working on shift is different, for there is no walking pure and simple but constant, noisy work, when every second of every action counts and your mind can never rest; a factory is definitely not like the countryside, with machines thundering so loudly you cannot hear the person in front of you speak. What is more, it is also stuffy and hot. After a shift is over a worker looks like a wilted vegetable, but then she still has to go on to a small group meeting and then on to class, so what strength does she have left for thinking? And I . . . all I could do was encourage her:

"Try to perk up a little, Qiaodi. After all, it is much better now than before Liberation when you had to work like dogs from dawn to dusk twelve hours a day!"

"You don't understand. No one was willing to work hard before Liberation. Half of those twelve hours was spent loafing about."

"This. . . ." What could be done? Suddenly I had

an idea and asked her loudly, "Are you awake now?"

"Eh? Yes, I feel better after that nap."

"Alright then, open your textbook and I'll go over the lesson with you."

From that time on I used to let Tang Qiaodi take a nap first and then keep her behind afterwards for a private lesson. She was very intelligent and made fast progress so that I was filled with hope for her, hoping that she, who had been through so much, would be able to open her eyes to the brightly-coloured realm of education.

Unfortunately there were times when Tang Qiaodi was not even able to take a nap. There were many political campaigns at that time when even production would halt and evening classes hardly counted! I became a sort of general factotum at the Party committee's propaganda department, working every day on preparing meetings, arranging rooms, composing slogans and writing summaries. As a symbolic figure Tang Qiaodi was even more actively involved in meetings and the little she had learned was soon forgotten. Nor was she the only one — all my students were reverting to their original levels. Whenever they heard there would be no class that evening it was as if they had been relieved of a heavy burden: "Oh good! Tonight we can rest!" Only a few were willing to come to the classroom. I was distinctly perturbed and went to the Party committee to object. The Party secretary was impatient with me yet could not say my objections were invalid. "Alright then, there aren't any meetings arranged on Saturdays. You can have them for your classes."

How could I possibly put up with giving only one

class a week on Saturdays? Tell me how I could possibly teach this way!

There was nothing else the Party secretary could do. "You tell *me* what to do! There will always be meetings, so you'll have to think of a solution yourself!"

The workers themselves objected to so many meetings, complaining that while the Kuomintang Party had been famous for too many taxes the Communist Party had too many meetings. They were remiss about attending them. The Party secretary wanted to correct the general attitude towards meetings but since it was difficult to criticize the working class he picked on me instead, saying at a large meeting,

"There are some people who do not take meetings seriously enough, even to the extent of opposing them and stressing the importance of their own work instead and asserting their independence from the Party! Culture, culture! Can you eat culture? Were the eight million troops of the Kuomintang defeated by culture? Tang Qiaodi cannot read, but does that mean she can't work or give speeches? Of course, it is better to be able to read."

All the people in the meeting turned to look at me. I kept my head lowered, my brain in a pandemonium, desperately hoping the ground would open up and swallow me.

Tang Qiaodi did not return to the evening school and thereafter always hurried past me looking rather awkward. Since I was still assigned to report on her progress I was often right behind her, listening to speeches she gave at meetings both at the Mill and elsewhere. Whenever she spoke there were always people constantly praising her, saying, "Well! It can't be easy for someone who's illiterate to speak so well. That's the working class for you!"

Tang Qiaodi also lumped illiteracy and the working class together, always starting her speeches with the words, "I am a worker and cannot read. Please forgive me if I make mistakes when I speak."

Whenever I heard these words they always made me feel rather uncomfortable — why was she unable to read? If she were able to read she could speak with even more depth and not just touch the surface, which also meant that at the moment my series of reports had nothing new to say and were being sent back to me.

I could not restrain myself from saying to Tang Qiaodi when someone was praising her, "Qiaodi, don't listen to this — you'd be better off finding some time for studying."

Tang Qiaodi shot me a surprised glance. "Didn't you get your fingers burned enough at that meeting?"

I blushed from head to toe and stuttered, "The Party secretary's in favour of literacy too — it's just that he doesn't want education to supplant meetings. Wait a minute. . . ." I had thought of a solution. "How about this — if you can spare half a day on Sundays I'll give you private lessons!" I knew that she now had a boyfriend so I only suggested a half-day, leaving her the rest to spend as she wished.

Tang Qiaodi chuckled. "What a man you are! What's the point? I can't read a thing but I'm still earning eighty yuan a month!"

Perhaps she meant nothing by this but it was nonetheless a considerable blow to me. It was true. In terms of wages Tang Qiaodi was earning the same as a shift foreman, the highest level for women workers, and with extras she could receive over eighty yuan a month. I was just a trainee, on the same level as a probationary technician, earning less than half Tang Qiaodi's wages. I dared not take away half a day from her — let her spend the time with her boyfriend, for those who had suffered so greatly needed a satisfactory marriage, a happy family and people's respect, for these combined added up to true emancipation.

At that time the female workers at the Tailong Cotton Mill were . . . in modern parlance, "doing very nicely for themselves". Their wages were all up in the sixty to eighty range, nothing very startling these days, but back then things were very cheap; female workers neither drank nor smoked and they did not eat very much either — a small three cent meal did them nicely. But just wait until they went into a big department store or fabric shop, for there their gestures and expressions caught everyone's eyes. A group of four or five, parcels under their arms, would walk down the street and everyone would know from their manner that they were from the Tailong Cotton Mill. A saying went around about them: "Marrying a Tailong Mill lass is like opening your own bank." These women workers' feeling of emancipation, their sense of glory and their enthusiasm for work were all so strong that you could almost feel the heat!

Tang Qiaodi's future husband was an experienced worker in an electricity plant. He earned more than she did and was several years older. He was a very open man but apparently had no ideas of his own and was content to follow Tang Qiaodi's lead in everything. The day they got married I bought them a small gift and went over to offer my congratulations. Their new home made my eyes bulge. An embroidered quilt, a big red wood bed and even a radio, an unusual sight in those days; they had a fourteen piece set of furniture which was far more impressive than today's "forty-eight legs" of furniture and less expensive. In those days families who had gone down in the world and speculators relied on selling their possessions to support themselves and there were loads of old furniture for sale. Who would want it? Capitalists were pretending to be poor, landlords and officials needed to sell too, and as yet cadres had not reached the stage of buying furniture.

Tang Qiaodi's marriage caused quite a stir at a time when an emancipated symbol was needed. Photographers came from the papers, the chairman of the Trade Union came to offer his congratulations and I wrote a long article entitled *Tang Qiaodi Stands Up*. My article gave a detailed description of Tang Qiaodi's house and furniture and enumerated the numbers of woollen garments and lengths of cloth stored in their camphorwood chests, for an accounting of this kind was an indication of emancipation. A symbol such as this had far greater powers of attraction for women workers than any evening class.

I did not raise the issue of evening classes again and when there were no classes to teach I did odd jobs for the Party committee's propaganda department. The Party committee was pleased with me and was preparing to bring me into the Party.

But then came the early summer of 1957 when I was stupidly over-zealous. There was a slogan at that time which said, "Care for others." It had come out in the early stages of the movement to help the Party to rectify itself. The Mill's way of caring for others was to make lots of cool, refreshing lentil soup and set it up outside the main entrance of the workshop so that everyone could drink some when they came off shift. When I saw the women coming off shift with clothes so damp with sweat they looked as if they had just crawled out of a river, I believed the provision of this soup marked a genuine desire to help others and revealed a respect for hard work, so I suggested that the matter should be publicized. It did not occur to me that the Party propaganda department would make a big fuss of it all by moving out all the evening class' desks and setting them up in a long line outside the workshop with several large buckets of lentil soup behind the desks and enamel mugs filled with soup on top. There was a long poster fixed along the desk-tops which read, "Be thankful for the generous gift of lentil soup! Give thanks to Chairman Mao and the Communist Party!" The Party secretary, the Mill head, the chairman of the Trade Union and other leaders were all there, tightly gripping ladles while a group of gong-beaters and drummers banged loudly and enthusiastically off to one side.

When the women workers came out of the workshop they were stunned, so much so that they dared not move forward. Furthermore, they felt embarrassed about eating in public. The Party secretary, looking stern, called out some names, "Mingdi, Laidi, come and have some soup — you'll work much better afterwards!" Mingdi and Laidi were so frightened by this attention that they hid behind other people. Only the young maintenance workers were unafraid, lifting up the enamel mugs, drinking and listening to the Party secretary as he talked; and when they had done they stretched out their arms and said, "Can I have another mug, Secretary?"

I could see things were not going well, so when I caught sight of Tang Qiaodi standing at the back of the crowd I turned and went back there to tug at her and said, "Go and drink some, Qiaodi. You should take the lead."

Tang Qiaodi pulled her hand away and said, "Go away! Do we have to bow and scrape just for a bowl of lentil soup?"

Later I informed the Party propaganda department of these general sentiments, believing its action to have been too extreme. Giving the workers lentil soup should have been to help them, not to gain their gratitude, and the way it was done only caused bad feeling.

Fortunately the leaders doled out soup for one day only and by the next day all the fuss and pomp had gone and it became very casual, with everyone happily drinking and hoping it would be repeated in summers to come.

In principle the matter was over and not even the head of the Party propaganda department had taken offence. Who would have guessed that disaster would strike? "The working class speaks up!" (As far as I knew, Tang Qiaodi and the others had certainly not said anything.) And I was involved too, my crime based on that mug of lentil soup.

I was "struggled" against.

"And why shouldn't you bow and scrape? Chairman Mao's generosity is higher than Heaven itself and you wouldn't be able to finish thanking him in a lifetime.

You are in opposition to the Communist Party and to Chairman Mao."

I said, "I am not in opposition, it's just because Tang Qiaodi said it that I felt it was over-doing things."

"Lies! You're slandering the working class!"

Tang Qiaodi did not feel that I had slandered her in any way so she stood up and ran over to where I was being "struggled" to try and clear things up. "Don't wrong him! I did say that!"

The members of the leading anti-Rightists' group pushed Tang Qiaodi away. "Be off with you now, go back to work. You don't have any education and don't know what goes on in intellectuals' heads. You didn't mean what you said but he's got hidden motives — he's against the Party and socialism and has been all along. He wants to be independent of the Party!"

Tang Qiaodi rolled her eyes in despair and tried to clear things up but she had no real notion of all the undercurrents involved.

Now I knew the advantage of no education — without education you cannot have any underlying motives, you certainly cannot stress the importance of your own job nor would you want independence from the Party — nothing can happen to you!

I was made a Rightist and sent to the workshop to do supervised labour. However, I still had a bone to pick with the head of the propaganda department. All these years I have worked hard for you, composing slogans, writing summaries, working late into the night whenever you wanted something the next day and then you do this to me — consign me to hell! Well, since the worst has already been done I can let off steam and say something.

I bumped into the propaganda department head in the street and tapped him on the shoulder. "People aren't made of stone you know, old friend. What did I ever do to you?"

The head blushed vividly, looked around to see if anyone else was there and then said, "You don't understand — there is a fixed quota for Rightists, and while there are lots of people working in our Mill, workers can't be made Rightists, the majority of cadres come from the workers' ranks and the old staff members just eat and don't open their mouths, so we only had you intellectuals to fall back on. Anyway, you wouldn't have escaped. To be frank with you, I didn't want to make you a Rightist and it was really hard to find someone who could use the pen for me."

When I heard this I sighed heavily. No one could be blamed but myself. When Tang Qiaodi and the others used to get into the Mill before Liberation, why did you stand and watch from your building? Why did you not follow them in instead?

The head saw how stunned I looked and patted me on the shoulder. "Don't be depressed. Work hard and if there's a chance in the future I won't forget you!"

Perhaps the head did not forget me, but the chance he spoke of did not materialize. I worked on Tang Qiaodi's shift as an auxiliary labourer until my sons had left primary school and had gone on into high school. They no longer remembered that I had once been a teacher but only that I was a Rightist because they had to fill in forms saying so each year. The people in the workshop certainly did not think of me as a Rightist, simply considering me a very competent auxiliary labourer, for they always saw how hard I worked

— I worked like mad! Was it because there were people supervising me? No, I wanted to work hard to transform myself, to get onto the right road. I fantasized that the blood and sweat of my labour would accumulate every day, build up day by day and increase in pressure until it would suddenly shoot upwards with tremendous force and knock the hat labelling me a Rightist off my head so that I would no longer be considered either that or an intellectual. I also dreamed of acting heroically in a fire (cotton mills catch fire easily) and being severely burned. And as I struggled to breathe, the Party secretary would come to see me and say, "Comrade, you are a true son of the working class!" I would be so moved that I would weep and not even regret dying! I used to have such fantasies before going to sleep and my tears would wet my pillow.

I always came to work early and left late, falling headlong into the fray the moment I arrived at the workshop.

Tang Qiaodi used to tell me discreetly to rest a bit and gave me all kinds of hints on how to ease up a little or save my energy. "Don't be stupid — there's no point in killing yourself!"

I was very grateful to Tang Qiaodi and admired her greatly, for while she had no education, nor did she think too hard, she always saw straight to the heart of any issue. And although I knew all this I still continued dreaming — I could not live if I did not dream!

Tang Qiaodi did not have a fixed place of work, but in a corner of the workshop she had a small office where the women workers who found it hard-going after three a.m. on the night shift would come to sit for a while. They were all so-called "little sisters", but their children were already in middle-school. Tang Qiaodi often used to call me in to have a cup of tea and a chat. All those with *di* in their names always used to like talking about their youth, how full of energy they had been, how actively they had worked, how doing the night shift had been as easy as blinking, no effort at all, and how the next day they used only to need sleep in the morning and still be able to go off in the afternoon to see a Shaoxing opera! And all the while they talked they would rub their arms and yawn.

Tang Qiaodi would talk about her youth too and sometimes mention me: "Hey! Do you still want to help me study?"

"Huh! If I'd known then that you'd be sitting here chatting I'd never have let you off like that!"

Tang laughed out loud. "Luckily I was never taken in by you! There was one of us girls who went off to study at the Worker-Peasant Crash Middle School, oh bother! My brain's no use . . . what was her name? Something *di*. . . ."

"Gendi," prompted someone beside her.

"Right! Tong Gendi! Well, Tong Gendi became some kind of technician but she had a hard time of it in '57. It's best just to quietly get on with your job, do a bit more if you can and if you can't, ease off a bit. My two sons don't want to study and my old man's angry about it. What's he got to be angry about? Let them stay at home, do some cooking and look after their little sister. They can go out to work later and we'll have saved on their tuition fees!"

Several other "sisters" agreed. "That's right! Just look at those people's kids who have graduated from university — their wages are nowhere!"

Tang Qiaodi swept me a glance. "Yes, just ask him sitting here!"

"Qiaodi, you earn a lot; can you spare me some?"

"Not at the moment — we've got some old debts we still haven't cleared."

"You've got old debts?" asked someone disbelievingly.

The person beside her affirmed this. "Yes, that's right. She bought a large house in the spring with a front and a back part, two side wings and a courtyard in the middle. And even though it's so big it only cost 1,200 yuan!"

"You must have stolen it!"

"No I didn't! The owner was afraid of a reform movement against private ownership, so he wanted it off his hand, but most people didn't dare buy it for fear of stirring up trouble. I'm not scared — they won't dare 'reform' me!" She looked at her watch and pursed her lips at me. "Hey, Mr Literacy! Time's up! Get back to work now. Ah! It's all very well being literate, but it's the seed of disaster."

Tang Qiaodi was absolutely correct — the disaster of education was worse than any car crash, for not only was it arbitrary but also prolonged. I shall not mention all the events of the "cultural revolution" — it was hard enough to bear dealing with investigations into reactionary slogans or a certain case! The suspects were always those with an education above middle school level, about forty years of age and with a strong sense of hatred for the Party and socialism. I didn't think anyone really hated the Party, but the other two points were so obvious, like lice on a scabbed head, clearly visible. I was put through the mill like everyone else and could not go home because I had to confirm times, have my handwriting checked, supply an alibi and attend meetings. Tang Qiaodi did not go to meetings and when she picked up her small bag in preparation to leave an unthinking official once cried out, "Hey, Tang Qiaodi! Why aren't you coming to the meeting?"

Tang Qiaodi tossed her head. "You're crazy! I can't read a single word and you want me to attend a meeting? Huh! Was that reactionary pamphlet written by an illiterate?"

"Oh! Yes, you go home! Go home!"

Thus the word "illiteracy" became protective covering — a bullet-proof vest!

Unfortunately I was defenceless and in a vulnerable position wherever I went. In the winter of 1969 I was once more the victim of a movement to "clean up the rubbish of the city", and this time my wife and children were affected too — the whole family was sent off to the countryside.

Just before we left, Tang Qiaodi and the others came to see me, their eyes filled with tears. When they saw how miserably shabby the family was several of them had a discussion and then bought my two sons a padded overcoat each and me a woollen hat, the kind old men wore, because they knew how strong the winds could be in the countryside.

The propaganda department head did not come to see me, but that did not mean that he had forgotten me, just that the time for that "future chance" had not yet arrived. Not long after the fall of the "gang of four" he came to the village to find me, expended a great deal of effort in getting me transferred back to the Mill, helped me be rehabilitated and gave me the rank of director of a vocational part-time school.

I was very moved and grateful but was not at all enthusiastic about teaching. I felt that workers should just get on with their jobs and that not everyone needed to be an engineer or technician or whatever. There was something else that made me very sad — most of the *dis* had retired, some of them having reached retirement age and others retiring early to let their children take over their jobs. Tang Qiaodi had also retired to allow her youngest daughter take her place. Her daughter's name was Jin Yunyi, a slim and beautiful girl who also worked in the fine yarn workshop.

My teaching work was comparatively straightforward. As soon as it was evening the classroom would be filled with lights and a mass of heads, all of them young. I never saw Tang Qiaodi and the others back there again — a generation had quietly slipped by; as a teacher I felt I had not been able to do anything for them, and my heart felt rather empty. Fortunately their sons and daughters now sat before me and thus I felt a sense of new life emerging.

Jin Yunyi studied diligently and never missed a class. When I saw her I asked after Tang Qiaodi: "Is your mother well?"

Jin Yunyi nodded.

"She doesn't object to you studying?"

Jin Yunyi was extremely startled. "Object? She'd object if I didn't come! If I didn't show up one day she'd never stop nagging me."

What! What was up with Tang Qiaodi? Had she caught this new fever for studying and told her daughter to jump on the bandwagon?

"Do you intend to be a technician or an engineer?"

"Neither. I just want to improve myself a bit."

I rarely heard a reply like this and was very interested because I wanted to understand each person's motivation for studying. Yes indeed, I should go and visit Tang Qiaodi — it had already been ten years since I last saw her!

"Please take a note from me to your mother. I'd like to know when I can go to see her."

Jin Yunyi immediately waved her hand. "Oh no, please don't come; our house is much too small."

I laughed to hear such pleasantries from this child, for I had been to her home which had a large room at the front, three main rooms at the rear, two side wings and a purple magnolia growing in the courtyard. I did not have any classes on Saturday evening so I strolled over to Tang Qiaodi's house. It was an evening in early autumn and there was a hazy night mist in the streets. I had been along this road many times but now I felt rather at a loss, out of my element.

Tang Qiaodi's main gate was ajar and in the otherwise empty main hall there were seven or eight bicycles. In the centre hung a very dim 15-watt bulb. The main rooms at the back were brightly lit and a radio-cassette recorder gave out a tune that sounded like a frog croaking. I heard the sound of people's laughter, the frog croaking and someone beating time. I called out, "Tang Qiaodi!"

There was no reaction from the main rooms but I heard Jin Yunyi's voice coming from the east side of the main hall. "Oh, Mum! It's Mr Zhu, the teacher. He's here!"

I turned round to look — when I had entered I had not noticed a structure resembling an earthquake shelter to the east of the main hall. When Tang Qiaodi came out from inside I was astonished at her appearance. Her hair had turned white, her back was bent and her face wrinkled. Around her waist was an apron — it was really hard to imagine that she had once been a distinguished and famous shift leader!

Tang Qiaodi took off her apron and dusted herself down. "Oh, Mr Zhu, you came after all. I was thinking of going with Yunyi to see you! Please, please come inside . . . oh dear, there's nowhere to sit. Yunyi, go to the back and borrow a chair so that Mr Zhu can sit outside." The way she spoke was still the same, her voice hoarse and very lively.

I felt rather embarrassed and did not know what had happened to her. "Your . . . your husband?"

"Retired and gone off in a huff back to his old village, and if Yunyi weren't here I'd be gone too!"

"What's wrong?"

"Ah, I shouldn't bring it up. My two sons are no good — they're uncivilized and disobedient. When they got married they fought over dividing the house and came to blows, each of them determined to get his share. It was a bad situation. So in the end we let them have it all. So you see, now I live in this shed like a refugee!"

An argument suddenly erupted from the main rooms at the back — the thin voice belonged to Jin Yunyi. "Just let us borrow it for a while, we're not stealing it!"

"Borrow! You're always borrowing from us but you won't touch Younger Brother's stuff!"

A woman retorted, "Younger Brother is a sucker! Who knows where all that stuff in his home came from anyhow?"

"How rude can you get!"

"Crash!" Some glass broke.

Several people shouted out, "Okay, okay, don't argue; you should stick together. Come on, let's have some music!"

The volume of the recorder increased. Perhaps it had four speakers because the "wah-wah" noise even made the paper in the door-screens tremble!

Tang Qiaodi stamped her foot. "Come back here, Yunyi, you can't deal with people like that!"

Jin Yunyi, her face flushed, returned and spat out, "Riff-raff!"

Tang Qiaodi said impatiently, "Alright, alright! Mr Zhu isn't a stranger, please come in . . . sit on the bed."

Inside the shelter there were two small beds tightly crowded together and piles of things everywhere. The only things I recognized were two camphorwood chests I had described in my article *Tang Qiaodi Stands Up*.

Tang Qiaodi saw how my glance fell on the chests and sighed, "They divided or sold everything I had but it still wasn't enough for them, so we old folk have to give them each thirty yuan a month on top of that!"

"A son doesn't support his father. His children live off their grandfather too." I quoted a saying common among old workers.

Tang Qiaodi shook her head. "No, I don't agree. I should help them out if they can't get by — I don't want to take the money into the grave with me. But they're just squandering money. Today they want to buy some kind of a recorder, tomorrow they'll sell it to buy a scooter — and that's nothing more than a bike with an engine attached!"

"Then don't give them the money!"

"Don't give them money? You just try it! Without money they get up to all kinds of tricks — my eldest's been detained twice and one of these days he'll end up in prison! What a disgrace! A disgrace to the working class!" As she said all this Tang Qiaodi was scrabbling through a drawer looking for cigarettes. She passed me a crushed-looking pack. "Well, you're better off — have both your sons gone to university?"

"No, one's at university and the other's in a factory. Both of them often talk about their Aunty Tang who gave them overcoats when we got sent to the countryside."

Tang Qiaodi smiled and said to Jin Yunyi, "You see how polite other people's children are. Kids from an educated home are different!"

I shook my head. "Not necessarily. Some are just as bad."

"Well of course, the fingers on a hand are all different sizes, but I do know that the parents of the kids who mix with those two precious lads of mine are all workers."

Jin Yunyi objected, "I don't want to be lumped in with them!"

"Of course you're not the same — you've had some education and go around with a book in your hand all the time; your head's always in a book."

"Education!" flared Jin Yunyi. "It's all your fault! You told them not to study, saying that an illiterate earns eighty yuan a month!"

Tang Qiaodi looked as if she had been scalded and flung out her hand. "Alright, alright, it's all my fault, completely my fault! And yet perhaps I'm not to be blamed totally, because who wouldn't have been wary with the intellectuals being treated the way they were?"

My heart went cold, for I had never thought that Tang Qiaodi's problems could be connected to the troubles that had faced "stinking" intellectuals. Now these troubles were being rectified and I had already been rehabilitated, but what of Tang Qiaodi? The propaganda department head could not help her and neither could I. All I could do was to look towards the next generation and ask them to forgive and understand what we underwent.

"Oh, Yunyi, you mustn't blame your mother! That's not right! Today you see me lecturing and I'm somebody but you didn't see me in the days when I was like a lost soul."

Tang Qiaodi was not comforted by this and shook her head. "No, I was wrong. You wanted to help me study back then but I ran off. Mr Zhu, my time's past, so please do what you can to help Yunyi — that's all I hope for!" Tang Qiaodi began crying. . . .

I left. Tang Qiaodi escorted me to the main gate and stood under the streetlamp there, waving and wiping her tears on the edge of her apron. After walking on a bit I turned to see the white-haired Tang Qiaodi still standing there in the hazy lamplight. Go home, Tang Qiaodi, I know you have faith in me; let me take it with me on the road before me and I will be able to go on for ever.

December 1980

Translated by Ralph Lake

The Man from a Pedlars' Family

TO speak of pedlars and well-born families in the same breath is a little unusual. Perhaps we're being a little too literal here. Let's just say that there is a certain Zhu Yuanda whose family from generation to generation has been engaged in peddling. During which dynasty did his family begin to peddle? It has never been ascertained. What things did they peddle? This too can't be said for certain. All I remember is that, thirty-two years ago, the day after I moved to this lane, just after dusk, I heard the sound of a bamboo clapper approaching from a distance. The rhythm was very marked. "Duo duo duo, duo duo, di di di duo, duo duo, di di duo." Although there were only two notes, there were many variations in modulation and in the strength of the tapping. Under the cover of night it seemed as though someone were calling or relating something.

I opened the long window facing the street, and looking down I spotted a light at the end of the alley. The light wavered on the white chalk walls, whizzing along like a spirit on night patrol. Gradually it became more distinct. It was a brightly lacquered *wonton* carrying pole. Steam was rising above the pole, while sticks of firewood burned in a stove. The pole carrier was Zhu Yuanda. At that time he was perhaps seventeen or eighteen, tall and thin. Beside him shuffled an old grey-haired fellow — his father. His carrying days were over. He'd very recently passed the carrying on to his son. Now he went on ahead striking the bamboo clapper, leading his son along the bumpy road he'd followed in his life that had enabled him to sell enough *wonton.*

In those days I was out of work. I relied entirely on helping several overworked Chinese language teachers, correcting students' composition exercise notebooks, getting a share of "classroom chalk dust" so as to make ends meet. This was not easy work and every night I was burning the midnight oil!

The "di di, duo duo" sound of that clapper passed nightly beneath my window. It would always depart at dusk and eventually return, most often just as the Beijing opera goers were leaving the theatre.

Whoever works through the long winter nights dressed only in a thin shirt becomes frozen stiff with only his shrunken heart continuing to beat. Inside the room there is no stove, while outside the north wind cuts through the window lattice like a sharp knife. The swirling night rain is turned into ice crystals which dance on the roof tiles. After midnight the whole world becomes an icehouse. At that hour, a steaming hot bowl of *wonton* dumplings for five *fen* with which you can have extra helpings of soup and hot sauce is a powerful temptation and a delightful pleasure!

Almost from the first day I became Zhu Yuanda's main customer. Later it became my habit that at the last sound of the Beijing opera gong, I would lift my eyes from the students' exercise books and wait to hear the warming sound of the clapper.

Zhu Yuanda's clapping was better than his father's. It was livelier and seemed at once both joyful and mischievous. Before long the clapper would be sounding beneath my window. "Eat, eat, come quickly and eat," it seemed to be calling. If I was a little slow, Zhu Yuanda would put down his pole and call up to me,

"Mr Gao, come down and warm yourself."

I would hurry downstairs to stand by his carrying pole, watching him fan the fire in the small oven and put the *wonton* in the pot while I listened to Zhu talk of the evening's business. He was very talkative; the words would flow in a stream, so that while you waited for your *wonton* you didn't feel the least lonely or anxious.

"Tonight's business was very good," he would invariably begin, as though sales never went poorly. "When the opera ended at least twenty people gathered around my carrying pole. And would you believe it, there wasn't enough meat stuffing. I'm not kidding you. The last few bowls had dumplings which were only half-stuffed. . . . Oh! Yours I set aside specially. They're stuffed with meat." He used a brass spoon to stir the *wonton* in the pot so as to prove this to me. "See, each one is bulging with meat."

I laughed as I said, "I don't care whether they're stuffed or not, just add a few more hot peppers!"

Zhu Yuanda didn't miss his chance to add, "It's so cold. Would you like another bowl?"

"Okay. But you're sold out of meat stuffing."

Zhu laughed heartily, his eyes winking slyly. "It would be throwing away your capital if you were to sell *wonton*! When you're doing business, you've got to say that there's a limited supply of your product. Then people will snap it up. If you tell them that there's no meat filling left, then the customers will want even the pastry sheets!" Saying this he withdrew from a little cupboard an earthenware bowl of meat which he thrust before me. "See if this isn't enough for you!" He laughed, thoroughly pleased with himself.

I began to laugh myself. It was just like watching a magician gaily and deliberately giving away the tricks of his trade.

At that time I didn't think that Zhu Yuanda was doing anything dishonest or that he was putting his profits ahead of everything else. I felt that the reason I wanted to correct more exercise books and he wanted to sell more *wonton* was because our lives were so difficult. Every night he brought me a little warmth. If I was able to buy for his sake once more bowl of *wonton* we would be helping each other out like two fish in a drying pond trying to spew foam on one another.

After Liberation I got a job as a cadre in an educational department. Although I was still busy, I didn't have to stay up half the night. Although my salary wasn't much, I felt it was beneath me to be having *wonton* dumplings at five *fen* a bowl. If I was returning home late from a Beijing opera, I would rather have noodles and shredded pork at fifteen *fen* to say nothing of sitting ostentatiously in a restaurant than to be eating tiny *wonton* dumplings standing with hunched shoulders by the seller's stall.

Although the sound of the clapper would still pass nightly beneath my window it lost its sense of mischief and joy with the passage of time, though it still seemed to be calling, relating something. And I rarely ran into Zhu Yuanda. When he'd return home late at night striking his clapper, I would be deep in sleep. If I did by chance catch that "duo, duo" sound, it would still be a feeling of warmth in my somnolence, though it would be very faint and far away.

It was probably sometime after 1958 when being obliged to queue up at a noodle shop I suddenly recalled what I hadn't heard for a long time — the sound of that clapper in the dead of night. It seemed a shame, as though I was missing something. But ever since the anti-Rightists movement, I could hardly dare to keep up my old attachments. I had not only to convince myself of this but also others. Socialism required a certain uniformity. It wasn't proper to have capitalist pedlars roaming the streets late at night. I was happy for Zhu Yuanda. He'd already broken free of his shackles and leapt into the torrent of the Big Leap Forward.

But things turned out differently. Zhu was no longer beating his clapper but carrying willow wicker baskets through the streets and lanes sneakily and in a flurry. In the spring he sold red bayberries, in the autumn water chestnuts and lotus roots; in the summer it was watermelon. In the winter he would set up his stall beneath the eaves of a house and sell roasted sweet potatoes. Sometimes he would sell cabbage, soyabean sprouts, live chickens, fish or shrimp. You could never know for certain what he would be selling. If someone in the courtyard had an unexpected guest, you'd always hear the housewife quietly ordering her husband to "run down to Zhu Yuanda and see what he's selling". I never bought anything from him and I wouldn't allow my wife or children to go. I believed that buying his things was aiding the spontaneous rise of capitalism.

I recall that during the mid-autumn festival one year

the anti-Rightist inclination campaign became particularly heated in my department. I had just been engaged in a war of words with someone with a Rightist inclination. When I reached home, the moon had already passed its zenith. The scent of osmanthus flowers was floating everywhere in the city. The moonlight was like water. It felt very strange — the struggle was so intense while all around one everything was so delicately beautiful. It was as though the world was out of joint.

As I was crossing a little stone bridge, I suddenly noticed Zhu Yuanda at the other end of the bridge setting up shop. One basket contained cherry-red water chestnuts, the other tender white lotus roots. I stopped immediately. I really wanted to buy a few to take back with me. These are the traditional delicacies of the mid-autumn festival. I hadn't seen them for years. But I hesitated because before me wasn't a state-run fruit store but a black market stall.

Zhu Yuanda came forward. "Comrade Gao. Why don't you buy a few to take away with you? See, they're very fresh. You can't get these at the state-run stores. They've a few but they can't compare with mine. You could hardly call theirs red water chestnuts. They'd break your teeth. They're all shrivelled up and they stink!" He gave his basket of chestnuts a shake to show that his merchandise was as good as his words. He was as talkative as ever, still looking for ways to get his customers to buy.

But the moment I began to listen, something seemed wrong. His patter was exactly like that of the Rightists in my department. It was slandering socialism! I didn't want to be engaged in a "struggle" with Zhu Yuanda. But I had to say a few words to help better the man.

"You should watch what you say in the future. You'd be wise to get out of these little business activities as soon as possible. They're the roots of capitalism and they're all to be swept away very shortly!"

He was startled. "What! They even want to arrest us pedlars!"

"They won't arrest you, but sooner or later everything that smacks of capitalism will be abolished."

He began to laugh. "Relax. It can't be destroyed. There are people who want to buy and those who want to sell. If the state-run stores won't sell things, can you say capitalism will be abolished?"

"How can it be abolished! Chiang Kai-shek's armies of millions were swept away. They would think nothing of little shops and stalls like yours!" I had often used this gambit at struggle meetings. No one could resist its devastating logic.

Zhu Yuanda made a sweeping bow. "Of course, Comrade Gao, I'm an ignorant man. I know nothing of the ways of the world. I'll take you as my guide from now on." Saying this, he quickly shouldered his baskets and left as though he feared I would arrest him.

As I watched him stagger away from me, I felt a little regret. There was a taste of ashes in my mouth. Those years ago standing by his carrying pole eating *wonton*, how could I have thought that he would be swept away. We had formed a genuine affection. As Zhu Yuanda slowly disappeared, I simply couldn't understand how this great distance between us had come about.

I longed to run into Zhu again, to smile and nod my head at him, to say a few pleasant words to him to show that our friendship was still alive. Unexpectedly, it was he who came to see me. He carefully seated himself in my rattan chair and eyed the furniture approvingly.

"Comrade Gao, you're doing all right now. I can remember that year when you were sick and you asked me to bring up a bowl of *wonton* for you. All you had then was a plank bed and a broken-down desk. It was pitiful!"

I remembered this not without some grateful laughter. But I was thinking to myself, "Why has he come to see me?" To tell the truth, ever since the anti-Rightist movement, I had become afraid of keeping up intimate relationships with almost everyone, lest I stir up trouble where I would have difficulty defending myself.

But Zhu was very good at guessing your meaning from your face, so he quickly explained his reason for coming.

"Comrade Gao, I had no other choice. You're the only one I know who has a way with words. I've come to ask you to write something for me."

"Write something!" I was even more afraid of putting something in writing.

"A self-criticism."

That was better. I could do that for him. "What are you accused of?"

"Profiteering. What else could it be!" He said this very easily as though it meant nothing to him.

I sighed, "And selling at exorbitant prices too!"

"Actually you could hardly call them exhorbitant. I buy my shrimps at forty *fen* a catty and sell them at sixty. Take into account I'm up half the night running around for sixty *li* and all I earn is two or three yuan. I know you won't like to hear this, but you earn more than I do and all you do is sit around and shoot the breeze."

This made me very uncomfortable. "How can you make a comparison like that. We serve the people. You just earn money for yourself!"

He wasn't convinced. "I don't serve the people? If I don't serve them, how is that they have shrimps to fry?"

My goodness! This strange reasoning had to be refuted. I stood up and jabbing my finger at him said, "You serve the people when you sell at the proper price. It's profiteering when you sell at high prices. This is a very serious matter!"

Zhu suddenly woke up to the situation he'd gotten himself into. He was like a balloon with all the air gone out of it.

"Sure, comrade. But you don't understand business. You don't understand prices. If you're talking about quality goods at fair prices, well, the vegetable market doesn't have any. Those list prices they hang up there are just to fool you. They're lies!"

"How dare you! . . ." I had learned my lesson from our last encounter so I did my best to keep myself under control but in spite of myself I lunged forward blustering.

Zhu Yuanda immediately clasped his hands in the traditional manner of submission.

"Okay, okay. I won't say another word. Just please write the self-criticism for me."

For a moment I had him. "If you've done nothing wrong, what's there to criticize? I refuse to do it!"

Zhu grasped my sleeve; then from a pocket he pulled out a wrinkled sheet of paper.

"Don't be angry. I was mistaken. I'm a capitalist! Write what you like; dress it up a little! I've known you, old friend, since I was in my teens."

This softened me. I sat down at my desk and took up my pen. But I couldn't help asking him, "Can you guarantee that you won't break the law again?"

"I . . . I promise. I promise you I'll be a little smarter next time." He winked at me as slyly as he did in his youth.

I was compelled to put down my pen and say to him earnestly, "Look, you're very intelligent. You're a very capable worker and you can put up with a lot. Why don't you become a labourer or a shop assistant? Isn't that respectable work? Why do you have to slither about like a rat?"

His face darkened. He sat dumbly in the rattan chair, his arms folded across his chest. It was a while before he spit out, "I . . . I can't."

"Why can't you?" I drew my chair over towards him and began my analysis.

"Selfish thinking is the main cause of all trouble. It's the root of all evil. Capitalism rests on that. You have to be determined to reform. Naturally, it isn't easy to switch from doing everything for your own profit to looking after the common good. It will be a painful transition. Take us intellectuals for example; our reform is particularly painful."

He was startled. "You suffer too?"

"Painfully."

"No, no. Don't be polite. You and your wife are both cadres. You draw a hundred yuan a month. You don't have to worry about the weather. You get your salary every tenth of the month. If I could only exchange your sufferings for mine I'd be in seventh heaven!"

"Why . . . Why . . . Why don't you get a job? Workers. . . . Cadres. . . ." I was unprepared for his attack. I was babbling like an idiot.

"Get a job? Without knowing any of the tricks of the trade, how much money do you think I would earn in a month?"

"You'd earn about . . . about . . . about thirty or forty yuan."

Zhu jumped to his feet. "Comrade Gao, I have four children. And then there's my father and mother. Eight mouths to feed in all. What could I do with thirty or forty yuan? I'm not a despicable man, shamelessly thinking only of money, am I? You don't see my children crying from hunger. The old woman, her eyes full of tears. It cuts into your heart more painfully than a sharp knife. I'm . . . I'm ashamed of myself. . . ." He choked back a sob and wiped away the tears running down his cheeks.

It felt as though cold water had been thrown in my face. It was as though I had been standing at the top of a high building looking up at the wide and beautiful universe when suddenly I noticed beneath me a dark mire, destroying my lofty feelings and dirtying my beautiful picture. I didn't dare say anything further. All I could do was to erect a barrier in my mind: this was an individual and temporary problem. There was no way I could find an out for this individual and temporary Zhu Yuanda. Nothing I could add by way of consolation. I was obliged to write a hurried and confused self-criticism and stuff it in his hands.

From then on I released my wife and children from

their ban, allowing them to buy things from Zhu Yuan-da. I felt that Zhu couldn't become a capitalist. If I could be counted a member of the proletariat, then how could he, being poorer and more wretched than I, be considered a capitalist? During the difficult periods when the free markets were permitted, I rejoiced for Zhu Yuanda. At that moment I knew for certain that he couldn't be a capitalist. But right afterwards there was a movement to adhere to the principles of class struggle. Then I would be confused. He really was a capitalist! I was in a terrible muddle. And then a thunderclap split the earth. The bugles of the "cultural revolution" were sounded, announcing the end of all capitalism!

It was altogether unjust. Now it was my turn to be publicly criticized and denounced because I believed that one should work hard for one's monthly salary, not always be spouting jargon, and that each person must make up his own mind. This had become pushing an extremely reactionary capitalist line. I was angry. Fine. From now on I would be indistinguishable from the masses. I would be like everyone else.

I mingled with the crowds. I read the "big character posters", watched the search and seizures, the public denunciations and the parading through the streets of the accused. When I had seen a lot of this I grew alarmed — this was no way to live. It was better in the small lanes where it was a little more peaceful. There life flowed on like a river. So every day I avoided the big streets and chose instead the laneways.

Little by little the big character posters began to appear there too. But they weren't very striking. The paper was rather small and the characters were all higgledy-piggledy. It cost so much effort to read these posters that one paid little attention to them. Later when I did look at them more closely I realized how strange their contents were. There wasn't anything like "reactionary capitalist line", "horrifying massacre of the oppressed" or "cruel suppression". They were all down to earth. Who had beaten whom? Who had thrown dirty water into so-and-so's courtyard? Who had had a child out of wedlock and with whom? Who was having a love affair with whom? They employed the most awful language. And they used terms like "ruthless" and "shameful".... My heart sank after I read them. It was as though I had been watching countless people pulling at one another's hair and thrashing one another. And it was all for nothing. Sooner or later there would be a verdict on the political questions, but how could all this feuding ever be settled? I had no appetite to continue reading. I turned and started east, passing in front of Zhu Yuanda's door.

It was wide open. There wasn't a rear window so the interior of the main room was dimly lit. I was suddenly given a terrible start. Standing on a bench in the poorly lit room was Zhu Yuanda, his arms hanging at his sides, his head lowered as though he were suspended there from something. His head was half shaved, his left cheek a dark purple, his eye above swollen to the size of a walnut. Next to the door had been stuck up a sheet of white paper on which was written, "Evil Den of Capitalism — Zhu Yuanda must bow his head and admit to his crimes! He has twenty-four hours to turn over the offending tools!"

He didn't notice me. I didn't dare watch him any longer because I didn't know to whom he was obliged to confess his crimes. Was it to me? Although I hadn't the skill to mend the heavens, I felt a twinge of conscience.

I skipped quickly passed Zhu's house. I looked about again and noticed the white sheets of paper next to the doorways of the flatbread pedlar, the hot water hawker, the itinerant barber and the cobbler. The contents of the texts were the same and they all bore the signature, "Combat Unit to Smash Dens of Evil". I felt that something terrible was in the air — that Zhu Yuanda had landed himself in a dreadful fix. The "cultural revolution" was bent on digging up all the bad soil of capitalism. If it didn't uproot Zhu Yuanda, then who would it?

And so it happened. Twenty-four hours later along came a gang of the "evil den smashers". Some were carrying iron clubs. Others, in imitation of the wandering knights of old, had great shining knives at their waists with a piece of red silk tied at the handle. The children of the lane followed closely at their heels shouting, "House search. Come and watch the house search!"

I hesitated a long while upstairs. Should I go and watch or not? According to the self-protective "principles" of the times it was best not to get involved in such questions of right and wrong. But I had to take a look. They were going to a poor pedlar's house; what could they confiscate there?

By the time I arrived the combat unit had already gone into action. This wasn't like the search and seizure of a cadre's home nor like that of an intellectual's. When they searched those places the emphasis would be on the "four olds", documents, letters, diaries, manuscripts and things like that. And those whose homes were being searched would stand silently to one side, sadly and indignantly watching the work of a lifetime, precious keepsakes, the wisdom of mankind all go up in smoke. And as the incarnation of evil did its work, it did so draped in a solemn cloak.

But the search and seizure at Zhu Yuanda's house was altogether different. That scene was absolutely terrifying. Even from a distance you could hear the crying and the wailing, the sound of things being smashed and torn and the shouting of the morale boosting slogans.

Zhu's house had become a battle ground. Inside, the din was deafening. Clouds of dust were being blown outside. The willow wicker basket was tossed outside and hacked to pieces by the great knives. This was because it had been an instrument of crime. It had been used to sell chestnuts and lotus roots. Neither did the vegetable basket escape. It had been used to carry fish and shrimps. One after another pots and basins flew out the door and were smashed to smithereens on the stones of the street. These things had all been used in making bean sprouts. For some unknown crime a tin bucket was battered by an iron club. Zhu's wife and children would shriek everytime an item was snatched up. The wicker basket that the children clung to so desperately was something that had kept them alive. Zhu's wife hugged the earthenware bowl. Inside were green beens she had been keeping to sell. There was a great cacophony of sound as they fought, bleeding and rolling around on the ground. I couldn't believe my eyes. How could such a noble theory produce such piracy as this!

Finally the *wonton* carrying pole was dragged out.

Zhu Yuanda was pursuing it like a madman. "Help! Spare that thing!"

How well I knew that *wonton* carrying pole. It had always provided warmth and a full stomach and it had never committed a single crime. On the contrary, it was a thing of exquisite workmanship. It was a miniature portable kitchen complete with cupboards, water tanks, wood shed, water canisters kept hot by surplus heat and storage compartments for salt, oil and spices. One could profitably study it in designing a galley for an airplane. I actually thought of walking straight over there and rescuing the priceless artifact. But I didn't have the courage. All I could do was stand and watch as the bamboo splinters flew under the blows of the great knives and the iron clubs.

Once the capitalist den was no more, it was all over. No one came and pestered Zhu Yuanda about a self-criticism. The storm passed quickly. But no one knew how he was going to make a living.

After dusk about three days later I saw Zhu's wife leading along their four children. There was a length of string in each of their hands. At dawn the five of them returned one after the other. Each had a great bundle of waste paper tied to his or her back. Those large character posters that had been pasted up all over the place had been quickly blown to the four winds and were being trampled into waste paper. By picking up enough of it, you could earn four or five yuan a day. So it's true — Heaven does allow a way out! Who would have thought that those posters that had driven men insane and others to suicide could have rescued Zhu Yuanda from the flames? Life is truly a mystery!

While Zhu was nursing his wounds at home, I went

to see him. He was as talkative as ever. He spoke a lot about the past. "Comrade Gao, I'm truly sorry. I should have listened to you in those days. During the Big Leap Forward my wife and I should have managed to get into factory work. You wouldn't have to worry about looking after the little ones, you just drag them to the union office and beg for help. The Communist Party isn't going to let you starve to death. Hell no! Why should I care about losing a little face. The skin off this face can hardly compare with money. Ai! I believed in myself too much. I always believed in bringing up my children by my own efforts. Things are fine now! My old woman and the children are out picking up garbage in the streets. . . ." Zhu's words poured out of him. It was as though he were giving me a summary of half his life.

There was nothing I could do but give him encouragement. "Calm down. First look after yourself. Later . . . oh yes, the *wonton* carrying pole was destroyed. That's a shame."

At that time the newspapers were carrying the resounding slogan, "We have two good hands. Let's not loaf about in the city!" The rumour was that it was thought up by a city dweller. I paid no heed to a slogan invented by some city resident. But I watched carefully if cadres were to be sent with their families down to the countryside. I couldn't allow myself to be found in such lists. So I was scurrying about looking for army representatives and workers' propaganda teams. This silent struggle was absolutely terrifying!

Very fortunately, I wasn't sent down. Zhu Yuanda came to say goodbye, his eyes filled with tears. His entire family had been sent down to the most wretched place. It was then that I understood the meaning of "We have two good hands. Let's not loaf about in the city!" Who was it that was loafing about in the city? Of course those with no jobs. Zhu Yuanda could not be counted as having a job; he must then be in the loafing category. It was useless to try to turn to someone for help.

The two of us sat in silence. He regarded me with envy, I him with shame. I couldn't see in what respect I was stronger than he. I could avoid every disturbance. But for him there was no escape. Even if I couldn't avoid being sent down, my salary would remain the same.

Just before we parted, Zhu took something out of his bag and gave it to me. "Yesterday when I was cleaning up the mess I found this in a corner. It would be a shame if it were chopped up for firewood. I want to give it to you as a memento." As he said this he placed the bamboo clapper before me.

I received it in both hands. I studied it carefully. It was a semi-circular bamboo clapper about eight inches long. It held no secrets. But in Zhu Yuanda's palms what wonderful sounds it produced. It had been caressed by generations of hands. The sweat and oil had penetrated the wood so that it now had a deep black sheen like a bronze mirror. Zhu gave it to me perhaps because he wanted me to remember that he had lived here and that he had done a little something for others.

Zhu and his family disappeared from the lane. Their departure was very noisy. There was a great beating of gongs as the banner "Glorious Household" was pasted up at their door. How could an "Evil Den" be transformed into a "Glorious Household"? In the twinkling of an eye, an old chicken had been turned into a duck.

Four other families in the lane disappeared at the same time. One was the cadre's while the others were the hot water hawker's, the itinerant barber's and the cobbler's. These were all in the loafing category. From then on you had to walk a mile to get hot water; it took twenty days to get your shoes mended. The old men had to queue up in the streets for a haircut. The old women would start cursing then, "Damn those who said they were loafing in the city. Now they've gone off to the countryside to loaf. You can forget about getting hot water to drink. Old man, don't bother about getting your haircut; just keep it in a pigtail!"

I heard no news of Zhu Yuanda for eight years. It wasn't until this spring that I heard that his two sons had been called back for work and had both been assigned to a certain factory. Later I heard that Zhu had returned. He sent a message through someone explaining he wanted to ask something from me. The moment I heard this I knew it had to be the clapper he was after. After all at this time everyone was talking about "social service" and the "commercial network", "hot water vendors", "*wonton* carrying poles" and what have you. Zhu Yuanda had returned, so of course he'd be returning to his old line of work. I got the clapper out and wiped it clean. I held it in my hands. In the deep gleam of the wood it was as though I could see the kindling burning in the red earthenware stove. I thought I could hear the "duo duo" sound reverberating at the end of the alley in the dead of night. Then it seemed to pause before a lamp-lit window. Inside perhaps there was a university student, or a young worker devoted to his studies, or perhaps a weather-beaten old man. They all feel keenly how much time they've lost and how little knowledge they have stored up in them. Their efforts are not for themselves alone. Their lives too demand that there be others bringing them warmth and convenience. It's taken me more than twenty years to learn this elementary principle.

It was dusk once again when Zhu Yuanda knocked at my door. My wife and he talked spiritedly as they climbed the stairs. The sound of their voices and of their footsteps were as joyful and as playful as the sound of his clapper in his younger days. Youth itself cannot last for ever, but its spirit can be recovered.

"*Aiya*! Comrade Gao. I've been back now for over a month. I've been busy finding a home and applying for a residence permit so I haven't had any time to come by and see you. And we couldn't be enjoying this day if we hadn't gotten rid of the 'gang of four'!" His resounding voice and exuberant facial expression were completely out of keeping with his former self.

I was very happy. I felt that he really had managed to free himself from his awful burdens. "Sit down," I said quickly.

He took a seat in the rattan chair and took out a pack of good cigarettes. Each of us lit one up. He inhaled deeply. Then out poured the story of his eight years in the countryside. I knew this story full well. It had been no picnic. But as Zhu told it it all came off sounding like a victory for him. Even though he'd sold off all the broken furniture, he'd got a good price for it. When he was finished he cast an appraising eye over my place. He shook his head disapprovingly. "It's all the same. Why don't you make some changes?" There was a tone of contempt in his voice as he eyed my furnishings.

I laughed. "Things haven't changed but the man has."

"Sure that's obvious! If you don't change then how can life go on?" Zhu straightened his new clothes. "Look. Haven't things really turned out well for me? My two sons are back. They're in state-run units. The two girls are in the county now. In collectively-owned units. Then there's my youngest — the fifth; I want to see him go to university. Four iron rice bowls and one golden one. Everything's just right. And that iron club can't smash them!" Zhu laughed heartily. He was thoroughly at ease and pleased with himself.

I quickly put the bamboo clapper in front of him. "You'll be taking up your pole again. Congratulations on the reopening of your business!"

Zhu rolled his eyes as though he didn't get my meaning. Then his face reddened a little. He put the clapper I'd given him aside. "You . . . you . . . you're kidding me!" He was very embarrassed as if he was a sort of crude millionaire whose shady origins had just been exposed.

I added brightly, "No, not at all. It's permitted to go into business for yourself, now. You're needed. The people in the lane have been asking after you."

Zhu raised his head. "They still expect me to work my carrying pole?"

I thought to myself: Of course that precious work of art had been destroyed long ago. You couldn't fashion a new one overnight. "Okay, then sell sweet potatoes. The old folks love that sort of thing. You can't get them nowadays."

Zhu Yuanda grinned and gave me a sly wink. "To tell the truth, the labour unit also approached me about going back to my old line. I humoured them a little. I'm already working in a factory although I'm a little unhappy with the job. Originally I'd thought of being the doorman. But they sent me to the workshop to sweep iron filings. I do a little sweeping and I get by. It's far less trouble and worry than baking sweet potatoes." Telling me his little joke was just like the time he thrust that earthenware bowl of meat in my face.

I didn't feel the least amused. I just sighed. "Why? If you don't take up your carrying pole then your son won't either. That would be a shame."

"A shame? Where's the shame in that?" He got up and straightened himself up. "From now on I'm not taking a backseat to anyone."

"But you never did. You were serving the people."

"Still 'Serving the People'! That was petty capitalism! It was to be abolished! I nearly gave my life for that 'den of evil'!" He'd become very excited all of a sudden. His voice was trembling. He shook as he took out the pack of good cigarettes. "Come, let's have another smoke. Let's not talk about all those awful things. I came here today to ask you for some review materials to help my son, the fifth one, to prepare for the university entrance exams."

I was certainly not opposed to someone going to university. I got together some mimeographed materials and put them in Zhu Yuanda's hands.

He thanked me effusively, and then said he had to be going. He asked me over to his place sometime. "Come on. Don't worry that you'll eat me out of house and home. The five iron rice bowls are refilled every month!"

The door below creaked as it closed. Unconsciously I opened the large window facing the street. It was as though I was looking for some *wonton* pedlar coming along with his steaming *wonton.* It was as though I wanted to hear that "duo duo duo" sound sweeping along. . . . But there was nothing. There was just Zhu Yuanda with the mimeographs tucked under his arm slowly disappearing into the night. I had been a little disappointed. But I hadn't dared say so in front of him. In these past years I and others had hurt him. We had attacked so much initiative. In the end all anyone wants to do is to hold that iron rice bowl in his cupped hands and avoid trouble and worry. By the end of the month that iron rice bowl can never be very full. And the rice in the pot will never be enough to go around.

October 13, 1979

Translated by Ralph Lake

The Boundary Wall

YESTERDAY night there was a violent storm and a slight mishap occurred: The wall outside the Architectural Design Institute collapsed!

The collapse of the wall was not entirely unexpected. It was simply too old! In its hundred-odd years of history it had already collapsed and been rebuilt several times, but none of the repairs had been thorough and the result was that the thirty-odd metres of wall bulged and humped in sections of all different heights. It was likely to come down at any moment, let alone in the middle of last night's storm!

With the wall down things began to happen. Everyone felt the Design Institute had changed. It was like an old man who'd just had his front teeth pulled out: When he opened his mouth there was just a black cavern with nothing blocking the entrance, and his eyes and nose had shifted position too; or like a beautiful young lady suddenly turned into a shrunken-lipped old woman, ugly and awkward. But it was not just that it was an eyesore; the problem was that once the wall was down, this peaceful office suddenly found itself linked directly with the street outside. The innumerable crowds of pedestrians and surging tide of vehicles all seemed to be charging toward the office, and the incessant clamour that now lacked a wall to keep it out poured directly in through the windows that in the heat of summer had to be kept wide open. People had to speak much louder than before simply to make themselves heard, serious conferences were disturbed by unusual sights on the street, and discussions of current events would be diverted a thousand miles from the topic to idle chat about a traffic accident that had occurred somewhere. People were unsettled, their concentration was upset, work efficiency was low and they became easily tired. The demands were unanimous: Get the wall rebuilt fast!

Next morning at the brief daily meeting, the director of the institute, Wu, made simple inquiries about how work was progressing, and ideas on routine affairs were exchanged. Needless to say the moment everyone sat down they started to talk about the boundary wall. Since the wall had come down, things had gone amiss, when they came to work they had the feeling something was not normal, like the confusion of the year of the earthquake. Someone put it even more ingeniously and said when he came to work this morning he'd walked straight past the gate. Seeing the heaps of bricks lying all over the ground, he'd thought it was the construction site next door. . . .

Director Wu rapped the table with his ball-point pen:

"Okay. Let's discuss the question of the wall. Frankly, I knew long ago that it was going to come down. It's only been the lack of funds that has stopped it being pulled down and rebuilt long ago. But in fact it's just as well that it has collapsed. If the old doesn't go, the new can't take its place! Yes, we'll build a new wall. . . ." Director Wu took a sip of water, "But what kind of wall shall we put up? I'm no expert on construction, but I always felt the old wall was out of keeping with the character of our unit: like a master tailor wearing a tattered gown without any buttons. On principle the new wall must be original and unique, attractive and tasteful, must unify form and substance. . . . Let's hear everyone's opinions."

As far as the importance of repairing the wall went, Director Wu's introductory remarks were both overly solemn and somewhat loquacious. In fact all he'd needed to say was one sentence: "Everyone thinks about it — how are we going to fix the wall?" But that would never do; work at the Design Institute could not be oversimplified! The mention of construction invariably evoked a division into three factions: the modernists, whose special interest lay in research on modern multistorey construction, the conservatives, who found it difficult to think of anything but classical architecture, and an indefinable faction who would accept a *fait accompli*, but were opposed to all changes and frequently displayed tendencies of nihilism. Although Director Wu claimed he was a mere layman when it came to construction, he did, in fact, consider himself to be far from an amateur, for he understood a great many principles: He understood, for example, practical economics, what was attractive and tasteful, what was advantageous to production, convenient for everyday life etc., etc. How to convert principles into blueprints was not his problem, but he couldn't neglect his role as leader and so had to rouse the two factions to a debate in which they would both bring forth their construction plans. Director Wu would then select the cream according to his principles and pass it on to the nihilists to unify. This was because they had a notable peculiarity: When they couldn't reject something, they had a great flair for effecting compromise and were also able to convince everyone. This technique of turning hostility into friendship was really very profound. Although to begin with Director Wu seemed dilatory and hesitant, equivocal and wordy, in the end he would make one feel it was a case of a man of great wisdom appearing slow-witted, and one would appreciate his prudence and reliability. Rebuilding the wall seemed a small matter, but it was nonetheless construction work, and in addition it was going to be built right across the front door, so it had to be treated seriously in order to avoid possible repercussions.

Perhaps Director Wu's opening remarks had sealed people's mouths, for the factions who should have begun the skirmish were temporarily silent, unwilling to reveal their firepower too early.

Director Wu was not worried. He turned to a young man seated in the corner and asked with a nod, "Logistics Department Head, what do you think?"

The so-called Logistics Department Head was in fact Ma Erli of the administration section. According to the principles of literature, in depicting a character, one does not necessarily have to describe his face, but in the case of Ma Erli it is simply essential, for he had come to grief several times in recent years precisely because of this face!

Ma Erli's face was certainly not ugly or sinister; on the contrary it was very good-looking. It was a plump oval with clear white skin, rosy cheeks and dimples when he smiled. His bright black eyes were particularly lively. Not bad, eh? If he'd been a woman he could have enjoyed its benefits for a lifetime. But unfortunately his face had got its sexes mixed and found its way on to the shoulders of a man, and the thirty-seven-year-old Ma Erli, an extremely capable and efficient administrator, had found himself with a baby face that did nothing to inspire people's confidence in his abilities! It was said that he was a victor in the field of romance, but when it came to some critical juncture, he invariably lost out. The sight of him filled some of the leadership with misgivings, they doubted that he could stand up to hardship and were afraid that he wouldn't be reliable in his work. And neither fear was completely groundless.

Ma Erli was always immaculately dressed. Even when he was going to the suburbs to plant trees, you wouldn't see him in sneakers or cloth shoes. He did as much work as anyone else, but there was never a speck of dust on his clothing. This roused the suspicion that he'd been dawdling. If he'd worn working clothes and leather working shoes, army pumps or straw sandals all day and paraded up and down in them, the results would have been quite different: "This man is prudent and experienced, hard-working and plain living." Even if his work had been mediocre, they would have commented: "One's ability may be limited, but what counts is his attitude to work."

There were also grounds for believing that Ma Erli was not a steady worker. Reliability is often a synonym for slowness, but Ma Erli seemed unduly agile. He was like the wheel of a bicycle — set it in motion and it goes flying.

"Xiao Ma (or 'Little Ma', as everyone called him), two window panes have been broken; you'll have to do something about it."

"Okay. I'll fix it straight away."

Word was given in the morning and that same afternoon the new glass was fitted in place. No one could resist going and poking it with their fingers to see whether it was in fact cellophane, because although it was easy enough to go and buy ginseng, to buy a plate of glass was a difficult operation: even if he had been lucky enough to find some glass to buy, how could he have got the glazier to come and put it in straight away? There it was nailed in securely with the cracks puttied over. . . . Oh no! They were just putting up a building next door! Don't say this slick customer had waited till they'd gone to lunch and then seized the chance to. . . .

Naturally all misunderstandings are cleared up sooner or later, but the cost is reckoned in time. Ma Erli had previously worked in the Housing Administration Bureau. In his first year everyone had kept a wary eye on him, afraid that this sharp-eyed, nimble-fingered young man was going to slip up. The second year they discovered that he was extremely capable, but had to be kept tight control of. Capable people were frequently liable to go beyond the limits of what was proper; it was virtually a rule. In the third year, he was lauded from above and below and all kinds of work was piled on his head. In his fourth year his leadets all declared that he should have long since been promoted to deputy section leader and should have risen one notch on the pay scale, but unfortunately the deputies' positions had all been filled, and pay increases had been granted two years ago. There, at such a vitally important juncture, Ma Erli really came off badly, and the fault all lay with that baby face!

The head of the Housing Administration Bureau was a kind-hearted old man who didn't like to treat his subordinates unfairly, so seeing that Ma Erli would have difficulty getting promotion in his own office, reluctantly parted with his treasure and recommended him to Director Wu. He told him how capable Ma Erli was and said there was no question of it, he had the makings of an administration section chief.

Director Wu agreed to take him on, but as soon as he saw Ma Erli he became suspicious. "Can this kind of person stand up to hard work? Will he be reliable?" The unfortunate Ma Erli began his second round of being tested. . . .

Director Wu had asked Ma Erli to speak first, on the one hand to get everyone talking and on the other to test his basic training and his experience in running affairs. So he slightly inclined his head towards the young man and said, "Logistics Department Head, what do you think?"

As expected, Ma Erli didn't know how far he should go. On the basis of his work experience and personal affiliations at the Housing Administration Bureau, he briefly considered the bricks, mortar and labour required and said, "No problem. I can guarantee that wall will be up within a week!"

Director Wu gave an "Oh!" of understanding. He knew from experience what was going on in Ma Erli's head.

"You can't just consider the bricks and mortar; you have to think of the significance of the style of the wall to the character of our unit."

The word "significance" opened the floodgates and everyone began to discuss the significance of the wall, but their intentions went far beyond the question of the wall.

As expected, the topic was taken up by the erudite scholar of classical architecture, Huang Daquan. This old chap was a little naive, but there was no need to guess at his meaning.

"I raised this problem several times very early on, but unfortunately was unable to attract the attention of certain people. . . . The collapse of the wall this time is a profound lesson to all of us. In the course of past planning, we never placed enough importance on it, never imagined that a trifling wall meant the difference between creating motion and creating stillness, meant creating a sense of security and unity. Now it's become obvious that the wall not only has functional value, but has a rich decorative significance too. Its place in giving a unique style to a group of buildings is of tremendous importance. Director Wu was right; this is a question of how to unite form and content."

This speech seemed to have grasped the motives of the leader, but it was in fact made with a definite object in view. He first pointed out there were means to reach that object but was willing to let other people use them. He had his own partialities, but he didn't want to enter the fray. The moment the words were out of his mouth, everyone's gaze turned quietly eastwards.

On a long sofa in the east of the room sat Zhu Zhou of the modernist faction. He was holding a teacup in his hands, watching the speaker with fixed concentration and listening with respectful attention.

Huang Daquan's words flowed smoothly on without a break:

"As far as traditional architectural artistry went, our

forefathers really understood the wonders that can be worked with a boundary wall. There are at least a dozen different kinds of walls — flowery walls, white-washed walls, grey brick walls, high walls, low walls, open-windowed walls, 'wind and fire' walls, screen walls, hundred pace walls, cloud walls, dragon walls — each kind of wall had its functional and aesthetic value. Most ingenious was the open-windowed wall; it not only created a division between motion and stillness, but could create stillness within motion and motion within stillness. It limited men's bodies but not their eyes. It's true to say that without a wall, there's no such thing as a group of buildings. A deep courtyard must have a high wall, otherwise where's the deep courtyard? Think of the Daguan Garden in *A Dream of Red Mansions*. . . ." Huang Daquan had got himself roused and unintentionally wandered into the garden of the classic novel.

Zhu Zhou, sitting on the sofa, put down his teacup and immediately launched off from the Daguan Garden. "Please note, we are not faced with the task of building a Daguan Garden. If we were about to restore the Old Summer Palace, Lao Huang's ideas would be worth consideration, but even then they could only be considered in part, because the style of the Old Summer Palace wasn't the same as that of the Daguan Garden. We have to consider this question from the point of view of practical realities. Although classical architecture has a very romantic flavour and can make us respect and cherish our own ancient culture, it's not feasible for application in practical work. The urgent task in hand is to build five and six storey blocks; I don't see what significance a wall even ten metres high would have for a six storey block!"

"It has significance!" Having mistakenly wandered into the Daguan Garden, Huang Daquan turned back. He was not totally ignorant of modern architecture: "Even a six storey apartment block should have a surrounding wall, because apart from floors four, five and six there are also floors one, two and three. The boundary wall is chiefly for the benefit of the first two floors. The fourth, fifth and sixth floors make use of space to create the difference between motion and stillness, but the first and second floors use the wall to create an impression of distance."

The battle array of the adversaries lay exposed and the rest of the debate continued in phrases and sentences with no more lengthy exposition. It had become hand-to-hand combat.

"Please state clearly the distance between a building and its wall. There's really not that much space in a city."

"If the wall is right next to the windows, doesn't it block the air and sunlight?"

"Build an open-windowed wall."

"Open-windowed walls are 'motion within stillness'. Aren't you contradicting yourself?"

"They are also 'stillness within motion'. You didn't hear that part of it!"

"Just a minute. Please work out the costs for your open-windowed wall." The speaker pulled a calculator out of his back pocket.

Director Wu immediately rapped the table with his pen:

"Don't get too far off the subject. The important question is how to rebuild our own wall."

Zhu Zhou was not willing to surrender. As he saw it the conservatives had no way out and victory had to be followed by hot pursuit.

"We haven't got off the subject; this relates to the kind of wall we should build — whether we want an open-windowed wall or not!"

Director Wu was highly experienced in controlling meetings and never allowed anyone to throw off all restraints, so he immediately asked Zhu Zhou in reply: "In your opinion, what kind of wall should we build? Be specific."

"More specifically. . . ." Zhu Zhou was caught somewhat off guard because he hadn't got any specific suggestions and had only entered the fray for the sake of the argument. "More specifically . . . looking at the concrete situation, the wall has two main functions: one is to cut us off from the noise of the city and the other is to protect us. There's no one in the building in the evenings, only old man Hong who sleeps in the reception office and he's already getting on in years. . . ."

Zhu Zhou beat about the bush for all he was worth. He knew that the more concrete the proposal, the more easily it was attacked, leaving no room to defend oneself or escape.

Huang Daquan saw Zhu Zhou's predicament, looked at his watch and pressed him step by step. "Time's almost up. Where are the brilliant suggestions then?"

"To be more specific, the wall must be high and solid." Zhu Zhou had no choice but to reveal his ideas. But this proposal wasn't exactly specific either — How big? How tall? Made of what materials? He didn't touch on any of it.

Huang Daquan was too impatient. He immediately cut in, "So according to you we need a steel reinforced, eight-metre concrete wall topped by an electric fence so that we can all sample the flavour of a concentration camp!"

"That'll ruin our image irrevocably, people will shrink at the sight of it. They'll think our Design Institute is an army ammunition depot!" somebody chimed in.

Zhu Zhou was angry: "I didn't say we had to build a concentration camp wall. Steel reinforced concrete and an electric fence on top were all your additions. Really! How can we discuss the question like this!" Zhu Zhou raised his eyes seeking moral support and continued:

"High and secure is right; if you want to talk about style then we should have a tall, solid wall with sharp-edged glass or iron spikes fixed on top to stop undesirable characters climbing over."

"Sharp-edged glass is the stupidity of those country moneybags. It's the equivalent of telling burglars: You can climb in over the wall, but just be careful not to cut yourself on the glass!" Huang Daquan answered back sarcastically.

At this everyone laughed and the atmosphere in the meeting room eased a little.

He Rujin, not being a member of either faction, had sat there all this time not uttering a sound. When the debate was most heated he took no part, but now that things had calmed down he began, "As I see it, all this controversy is superfluous. If the boundary wall hadn't come down, no one would have thought of open windows or broken glass. Everyone felt it was perfectly natural and suitable as it was. Sure enough it's come down now, but there's not a single brick missing, so the most reasonable thing to do is to rebuild what collapsed. Is it necessary to embark on a large scale construction project? A pure waste of money! Our funds are limited; we should always put economy first. Besides, the history of the wall has set precedents for us to follow."

If this had been said at the start of the meeting it would have certainly caused an uproar, but it had been opportunely timed. Everyone had argued until they were dizzy and no one was able to offer a concrete proposal that was acceptable to everyone. Listening to He Rujin speak it seemed as if they'd suddenly discovered the truth: He was right; if the wall hadn't collapsed there would have been no problem. Now it was down, simply rebuild it in the old way. It was just simple logic and there was nothing to argue about. The two factions nodded their heads and smiled as if an unnecessary misunderstanding had just occurred.

Director Wu gave He Rujin a disdainful glance. He didn't agree with this kind of negative attitude. His principle was to build a new, original and unconventional wall to add a bit of glory to the Design Institute. But time was already up and it would be difficult to get any substantial results from further discussion — he had no choice but to lay the matter aside for the time being: "All right. We won't say any more about the wall today. Everyone goes away and thinks about it. The boundary wall is the exterior of the Design Institute. Things shouldn't be judged by appearances, but they can't be too ugly all the same. Please use your imagination; we want to build something unique. Meeting's over!"

Director Wu's words brought the two factions back to their senses. They felt that He Rujin's speech amounted to nothing; he might just as well have not spoken. Determined not to let He Rujin get away with it lightly, they chased him into the corridor and launched an attack:

"What you say sounds very masterly, old pal, but in fact it amounts to attempting nothing and gaining nothing."

"According to your logic, we can disband the Design Institute. Everything that already exists is reasonable. What is there to design?"

Director Wu, hearing the voices fade into the distance, smiled and shook his head. Turning his head he found that Ma Erli was still sitting in the corner by the door!

Director Wu was surprised: "What is it? You still have some problems?"

"No . . . nothing else. I'd just like to ask. . . . How *are* we going to rebuild the wall?" Ma Erli stood up, his large eyes opening even wider.

Director Wu smiled. He'd had the same experience himself as a lively and enthusiastic young man. Once there was something on his mind, he would itch all over as if he had lice, wishing that he could remove all his clothes at once. But in fact most of the time it was quite unnecessary. Impatience only spoilt one's appetite and if you didn't let the lice bite, you might be bitten by a snake. With your clothes off you might catch cold. That was experience! But it was not appropriate to tell all this to Ma Erli — one had to encourage the positive side of young people.

"How we finally rebuild the wall will be up to you. I've already laid down the principles and comrades have already put forward several good suggestions. You can make a plan based on that. Rebuilding the wall is the responsibility of the administrative section, so I'm putting you in charge." Director Wu patted Ma Erli on the shoulder, "Do your best. You're in the prime of life and capable of doing a good job!"

Ma Erli was not very familiar with the procedure of making so-called "plans" and wasn't sure how much of a gap there was between "plans" and concrete actions, but he was delighted to be "put in charge" and felt that Director Wu had confidence in him. He hadn't been misled by his baby face. Work well for those who understand you. From now on he'd work even more enthusiastically.

Even when Ma Erli wasn't feeling enthusiastic he got things done pretty fast, but once his enthusiasm was roused his speed was phenomenal. Nevertheless this time he was really in earnest, so he first sat down in the office and lit a cigarette while he thought things through. Before he'd finished his first cigarette, he was on his bicycle pedalling furiously towards his old work unit, the Building Repair Centre.

The Building Repair Centre was in a dilapidated old building that made one feel that there were numerous buildings in urgent need of renovation. Content and form really were unified!

Ma Erli had been pedalling at a good pace, so he arrived just as their daily conference was dispersing and the director of the centre, a technician and several work group leaders were just walking past the lime pool. Ma Erli didn't even dismount at the gate. From across the yard he waved a hand and shouted, "Comrades, wait a minute!" By the time people had turned their heads to look, Ma Erli was beside them.

"Oh! It's you!"

Ma Erli had worked at the Housing Administration Bureau for five years and was familiar with all the people in the Building Repair Centre. For some reason his baby face was always welcome at this basic level unit. Everyone looked on him as a lively, capable younger brother.

Ma Erli jumped off his bicycle still puffing: "Thank Heavens I caught you, otherwise things would have had to be delayed until tomorrow."

"Xiao Ma, heard you've been promoted. Congratulations!"

Ma Erli wiped the sweat off his forehead, "There's no need for congratulations, but if you're willing I'd like you to help me with something." He pulled out a pack of cigarettes and handed them round. "Let's sit down to talk — this isn't a simple matter!" To get everyone settled, Ma Erli took the lead and sat down on a pile of old bricks, not forgetting to protect his clean clothes by putting his hanky down first, despite his haste.

The technician sat down, and the director squatted in front of Ma Erli while the group leaders stood to one side smoking.

The director looked at Ma Erli with a smile, "Well, what is it that's got you so anxious?"

"It's not a particularly important matter — the wall at the Design Institute has collapsed."

"Is that all! You go back and we'll get it fixed for you — it's as simple as that." The director stood up. He didn't see anything remarkable in rebuilding a wall.

Ma Erli grabbed the leg of his trousers with one hand, "I asked you to sit down, so sit down. Listen to me. Fixing the wall is not so simple. The leadership has passed the job on to me. They want me to come up with some good suggestions. I'm hopeless by myself. I have to rely on you people to back me up!" He went on to explain all the details of the argument about the wall.

The director of the centre scratched his head, "This is not going to be easy. All *we* do is take responsibility for laying the bricks."

The technician smiled, "It's true, the Design Institute can't put up an ordinary wall. This is a question of a signboard."

Ma Erli immediately seized upon the technician and wouldn't let go. He knew this technician had a lot of good ideas tucked away and was soon to be promoted to assistant engineer. "Right! Right, old pal, whatever happens I'm going to ask for your help in this. Next time you have to do something that needs a lot of running around, just make one phone call and I guarantee that within fifteen minutes I'll be there." Ma Erli's words were pointed: The year before the technican's wife had suddenly taken ill and it was Ma Erli who had arranged the car to take her to hospital.

The technician prodded Ma Erli in delight, "Get on with you! Whoever sends you running around is sure to come to grief — not to mention the fact that this is quite different from calling a car. It's hard to do business with the people at your place; they discuss things for hours and can't even set down limits."

Ma Erli's eyes flickered as he thought. "You can't say that; there are limits." His brain really was agile, good at sorting the main threads of a tangled affair. "They have several fundamental ideas. The first is it must be solid."

"Of course. It would never do to put it up today and have it fall down tomorrow." The technician picked up a tile chip and began drawing lines on the ground. He was a man who emphasized practical results and was adept at converting all kinds of demands into a workable blueprint — thickness, length, a buttress every five metres — that would be solid enough.

"Secondly it must be a high wall, but not look like a concentration camp."

"Walls are usually the height of a man with hands raised plus 12 inches. There's no need to be higher than that." The technician wrote down "two metres high".

"Thirdly, it must include open windows etc., something attractive that lets the air through."

The piece of tile still in his fingers, the technician shook his head, unable to continue his drawing. "That makes it difficult. Open windows on top of a two-metre wall would make it too tall and a light top on a heavy base would not be attractive. But if the windows are less than two metres above the ground, the noise from the street won't be screened out and in addition you're just inviting passers-by to stick their heads in and have a look. Problems!"

Ma Erli waved his hand. "All right. Let's put that problem to one side for the time being. Fourthly, the wall must be burglar-proof, but can't have broken glass on top."

"Another problem!"

"We'll put that aside too. The fifth requirement is economy — it has to be cheap." Ma Erli patted the old bricks he was sitting on. "Hey! I can solve this problem. You can sell me the old bricks from your demolishing jobs. You can charge me a nominal sum for them — you usually have to *pay* to get rubble taken away!"

Everyone laughed. The old bricks piled here were all good grey bricks. Where was the rubble?

The director shook his head. "You're a sharp one. There's no easy deal that you're not into."

The technician was still puzzling over the problem points: "What! You still have more stipulations?"

"The general consensus is it's got to be original and unconventional."

"Well of course," the technician tapped the ground with his piece of tile, "the biggest difficulty is the open windows, where should they go. . . ."

A group leader spoke up, "Couldn't we put in hollow glazed bricks? We pulled down a great pile of them from old houses; they've been stacked over there ever since." He pointed to the west. "Look, if we don't get rid of them soon they'll be completely smashed to pieces."

The technician clapped a hand to his head, "Brilliant! Above one metre seventy-five we lay hollow glazed bricks — you've got your open windows and the wall's not too high. They're brightly coloured too. Lao Wang, go and get a block for Xiao Ma to look at. See if he likes it."

Lao Wang brought one of the blocks over. It was a

foot and a half square earthenware decorative block, patterned with hollows cut through the centre and glazed a deep sapphire blue. Blocks could be put together as required to form open windows of any size or shape. They were frequently found in the inner courtyard walls of old buildings.

Ma Erli was naturally highly satisfied. Where could one go to find this kind of thing nowadays? But he still had to ask the question, "We'll be petty-minded first and lofty-minded later. How much do these things cost each? If it's too expensive we can't afford it!"

"Eighty cents each. How about it — it's as good as giving them to you."

Ma Erli slapped his thigh, "Terrific! Here, have another cigarette."

The technician waved his hand, "Don't hand out the smokes; your knotty problems have already been solved."

Ma Erli pushed the cigarette into his hand. "What, thinking of slipping off? You haven't worked out how to keep the thieves out yet!"

The technician laughed. "Old pal, that is a problem for the gatekeeper to solve."

Ma Erli was not willing to let it go at that. "People and walls are two different things; you're playing around with me."

"Fine, fine, I'll stop playing around. Director, you come in on this. Your place was burgled last year."

The director of the centre had in fact done quite a bit of research into theft prevention. "Xiao Ma, do you know what a thief is most afraid of when he climbs a wall?"

"Who knows! I've never robbed anyone."

"They are terrified of noise. If you build a small roof on top of the wall with a roof ridge and overhanging eaves, then lay it with loose tiles, the moment your thief gets on to it the tiles will go crashing to the ground with a noise that'll have him wetting his pants."

"Great! Far more effective than broken glass — thieves all wear gloves nowadays!"

The technician took it up from the aesthetic point of view. "Right! Flat topped walls are ugly too. It should have a hat — like a bamboo hat." He stamped out the rough draft he'd drawn in the earth and used the broken tile to completely redraw the whole boundary wall topped with a little roof with curved ridges. Finishing the drawing he tossed the tile away. "Xiao Ma, if this wall isn't a great success all round you can write my name upside down on it and put two crosses on the name."

Everyone stood around the rough blueprint scrutinizing it carefully. The verdict was unanimous approval.

Ma Erli was also delighted, but not to the point of complacency. When he was doing something he liked to get everything settled at one go. If he was fitting a window, he'd never forget to buy the putty; building a wall, how could he leave it on the drawing board? "Hey, don't get too engrossed in self-admiration, first put it up and then see if it's so wonderful. When can you start work?"

The director did some lengthy mental calculations and then asked the group leaders the work situation at several work sites. "We can do it like this — we'll rush things along a bit and fit you in in fifteen days' time."

Ma Erli jumped up, and retrieving his handkerchief from the brick wiped his hands. "How will that do? I already made a guarantee at the meeting that I'll have it up within a week!"

The director gave a sigh of regret. "See, it's not surprising that people say you're not reliable. It's not as if you don't know that the Repair Centre is up to its ears in work — how could you make a guarantee like that?"

"I know the situation. I know it only too well. To tell the truth, if I wasn't fully aware of the situation I'd never have dared to make a guarantee. How about it? Can you find some way of organizing it for me?" Ma Erli took a stride forward as if he were going to force the director into the lime pit.

The director still shook his head, "There's no way. There's not enough time."

"All right. If you can't find a way, I'll arrange it. I'll give you three days' grace and you can start work on Saturday evening. Send the materials over in a truck that can take the rubble away and send a dozen labourers to clear up the foundations. On Sunday send over a good crowd of skilled bricklayers, all you old hands included, and we'll work all day and stop when we've finished the wall. You'll get overtime, an evening meal allowance, cigarettes ... it's nothing — I can afford four or five packs of cigarettes!"

"Ah ha! You're certainly asking us to do a bit of overtime!"

"What about it? Haven't you ever done overtime before? You're not expecting me to lay on a feast, are you?"

"That's ... that's repaying our friendship — half official, half personal," the director was forced to admit.

"We're doing this all in the public interest. I'm just asking you to save my face," Ma Erli sighed. "I'm just a person who loves to keep up appearances, but always has a hard time. Everyone's afraid I'm unreliable but I still simply have to be impatient to get things done. I've just been moved to a new post and if the first guarantee I make turns out to be an empty boast, who's going to trust me in the future? Help me out, folks." Ma Erli had begun to plead with them. People trying to get things done often had to pay obeisance to the powers that be. It was pitiful to see.

It was one of the work team leaders who first slapped himself on the chest, "No problem, leave it to us!"

"Smooth sailing, Ma Erli!"

The trivial but complicated problem of the wall was thus decided upon. From start to finish it took something like half an hour.

By Saturday evening, the staff of the Design Institute had long since finished work and gone. An electric cable was temporarily wired up outside the gate and four 200-watt light bulbs flooded the roadway in brilliant light. People arrived, trucks arrived, bricks, tiles, lime and glazed blocks were brought in and the rubble was cleared out. In four hours all the pre-construction preparations had been completed. Then early on Sunday morning, the work began with the centre director and group leaders all lending a hand. The technician took meticulous care to supervise every step of the way. Putting up the wall outside the Design Institute was the equivalent of working under an expert — you had to know the tricks of the trade. He scrutinized it from left and right, near and far, and even climbed up to the top of the office building to get a view of it from there. He checked from every angle to make sure the height was right and to decide where the glazed blocks should be laid so that the wall harmonized with the original building and was aesthetically pleasing from any angle.

The office was empty on Sundays, so Ma Erli flew around in a whirl of activity, even requisitioning the services of Hong, the old gatekeeper, to give him a hand. He made tea, proffered cigarettes and hunted out odds and ends in the way of nails, aluminium wire and cotton thread, when necessary making flying trips to the hardware store. Here they shouted for Xiao Ma, there they shouted for Xiao Ma and true to his name,* Xiao Ma would spring like a young colt over to whoever was calling him.

The boundary wall went up at an amazing pace. People chased around shouting and calling in a bustle of activity that evoked the astonishment of passers-by.

"They must be putting up a private house!"

"No, they're having a technical examination. It's a real test of expertise to decide their grade and level."

Laying the wall was pretty easy and if they'd had new bricks it would have gone up even faster. But the glazed blocks and little roof were not so easy, particularly the roof. It was delicate work and you couldn't get everyone up there working on it either. The tiles had to be arranged carefully ridge by ridge. After every foot or so, the tiles were placed to form decorative tops and allowances also had to be made for the dripping of rain water. They'd originally planned to finish work and then eat dinner, but in the end the lights were burning until eleven at night.

Ma Erli bowed and scraped and thanked them a thousand times. He saw everyone on to the truck and

---

* Xiao Ma literally means "little horse".

then took down the electric cable, tidied up the odds and ends lying about and swept the ground. He didn't feel tired and was so pleased with himself that he couldn't resist running over to the other side of the road to admire every detail of the masterpiece.

Seen dimly through the moonlight, the boundary wall looked enchanting. It was full of poetry with its white wall, black tiles and sapphire blue windows suffused with a sparkling brilliance. The light that shone out through the patterned blocks was transformed to a shining emerald green. A light breeze blew, swaying the tree branches and making the rays of light glimmer and dance as if there was a fairytale world hidden deep within. Above the wall one could see the black roof of the building inside jutting into the night air and the wall suddenly seemed to change, melting into one with the main building, whose style it matched to perfection. The nearby road had changed too; it seemed to be the entrance to a scenic area or cultural palace. The more Ma Erli looked, the more beautiful it seemed. He felt it was the most perfectly handled job he had ever undertaken. He didn't feel like going home, so he stretched himself out on a long sofa in the upstairs meeting room. He hadn't slept properly for two days, but this time he slept very deeply and very sweetly. . . .

The sun rose high in the sky and a ray of sunshine crept in through the eastern window and shone on Ma Erli's baby face. He was smiling peacefully, and the faintly visible dimples gave him a most attractive, naive, childish air. But he slept too deeply, for he didn't hear the exclamations of wonder and general hubbub that filled the courtyard below.

On Monday morning, people arriving at work were

stupefied by the sudden appearance of the boundary wall. Although everyone had hoped the wall could be speedily rebuilt, they hadn't been in the least prepared to see it up by today. If construction had been carried out under one's very eyes — adding a foot today and six inches tomorrow, with people coming and going and the ground littered with bricks and plaster, when it was finally finished everyone would have felt a great sense of relief that the chaos was over. Then regardless of the style of the wall, it would have seemed fresh and new to look at. Today, in the blink of an eye, old mother hen had turned into a duck and it was as if it had been stolen from somewhere and brought here in the night. They weren't used to it; it was too dazzling. But the vast majority of people blinked their eyes a few times and became accustomed to it. Everyone could see clearly that this wall was better than the old one, and far better than no wall at all. But there were also some people who looked it up and down and from side to side and couldn't set their minds at rest. Despite the fact that they couldn't specify anything particularly wrong with it, they still felt that it was a bit too "uhh . . . ." What "uhh" was, they hadn't really thought about and were even less capable of stating clearly. That judgement would have to await the arrival of someone with authority. Should Director Wu say "good!" most of the "uhh's" would disappear and the small number remaining, quick to grasp the situation, would praise the wall to the heavens!

Director Wu stood in the midst of the crowd looking at the wall, offering no comment from start to finish. He felt the boundary wall was what he'd imagined and yet not what he'd imagined. It was what he'd imagined because it was very unconventional, but not what he'd imagined because he hadn't envisaged *this* kind of unconventional. When he was asked to comment on the wall he just said softly, "Hmm, I never thought Ma Erli could move so fast!"

"That's just it, he's gone about this like a harum-scarum, didn't even bother to consult general opinion," someone immediately chimed in. He primarily felt that his opinion hadn't been sought on the question of the wall; it was really a bit too "uhhh"....

The three factions whose opinions had been solicited were also highly dissatisfied. Each felt that the wall had assimilated too few of their sound proposals. Their wonderful ideas had been messed up by unorthodox and wrong notions. They all stood beneath the wall explaining how it should have been done amidst much discussion and appraisal. Their ideas were concrete, penetrating and rich in humour.

"Call this a good-looking wall? Neither Chinese nor Western. Wearing a Western suit topped by a skull cap and with a green scarf wound round its neck. Which dynasty does that getup belong to? Does it have the slightest flavour of the modern age?" Zhu Zhou finished his appraisal and perused the crowd in search of support.

"That's right, a perimeter wall is after all a wall, what do you want to give it a great roof for?" The people who found the wall a bit too "uhh" began to express themselves more explicitly. All that offended their eyesight lay in that small roof. But in fact it could hardly be called a roof; it was just shaped like a roof, that was all.

Zhu Zhou was extremely complacent. He went over

to the wall to measure its height and rub his hand over the protruding brick pillars. He felt the height and solidity of construction were just what he'd had in mind. It was just that the open brickwork windows and that little roof were too preposterous. It was the conservatives who were the cause of them being there! He turned his head and called to Huang Daquan:

"Lao Huang! You should be satisfied this time — the flavour is entirely classical!"

Huang Daquan shook his head, "What are you talking about? He hasn't completely grasped the spirit of my conception. The roof ridge shouldn't be a flat line, it's too monotonous. He could have built two decorative squares in the centre to symbolize good luck; that would have been different without being too flowery. Why did it have to be so tall? . . . Lao Zhu, go and stand over there and don't move, I want to take a picture. I'll call it, 'Even with wings you couldn't fly away.' "

"You're right. It's too tall."

"There should have been corner eaves sticking up at either end."

"They didn't lay quite enough glazed blocks."

Everyone who had felt the boundary wall was a bit "uhh" helped to pick fault with it. Their ability to criticize had always been greater than their creative abilities.

He Rujin didn't make any specific comments on the wall, but approaching from a different angle brought up a question likely to have the masses rising in anger.

"Let's temporarily ignore whether this wall is good or bad. What I want to ask is does it conform with our principles of economy? How much labour did that little roof require, how much each were those glazed blocks? I'm afraid this will have used up every cent of our administrative budget. Our thrift bonus this quarter is likely to be twenty cents each!"

He Rujin's words evoked a wave of excitement, "That's right! He should have just built the wall and had done with it, why did he have to go and trim the top with lace!"

"This is just. . . ." The speaker glanced around and found no sign of Ma Erli. "This is just Ma Erli's work style. The man is wasteful and extravagant. By the look of it he's a spoilt young rich boy, spending money like running a tap."

"Director Wu, was it you who made him build it like this?"

Director Wu hastily waved his hands, "No, no! I just told him to think about it. I never thought he'd act first and then ask for approval. Ma Erli. . . ." Director Wu shouted, but Ma Erli was still sleeping on the sofa and didn't hear.

"Old Man Hong, have you seen Ma Erli arrive this morning?" Someone gave a hand to find Ma Erli. He wanted to call the chief offender to question there on the spot.

The old gatekeeper Hong was furious. "Stop your screaming and shouting! He hasn't rested for two days, unlike you!" Old Hong was disgusted by all the artful talk. He sided with Xiao Ma because he'd seen him working endlessly while the wall was being built, clothes soaked through. Not everyone could do that. Sitting at the gate he'd also heard the comments of passers-by — they all said how attractive the wall was. He personally had an even deeper affection for the wall, for from now on he could sleep in peace. If a burglar tried to climb in, some of the tiles on the eaves would go crashing to the ground!

Director Wu frowned. He waved his hands for silence and told everyone to go and get on with their work, at the same time calling Lao Zhu, Lao Huang, Lao He and others to attend a brief meeting upstairs.

Zhu Zhou pushed open the door of the meeting room and discovered Ma Erli sleeping peacefully on the sofa!

"Heavens! We've been looking for you everywhere and couldn't find you, and the whole time you were here having a good sleep. Get up!"

Ma Erli rubbed his eyes and scrambled up. Still half asleep, he hazily weathered the hail of criticism.

But it wasn't so bad. Although there was a lot of criticism, no one suggested demolishing the wall and rebuilding it. The boundary wall passed the summer and autumn unscathed. Delicate grasses began to grow around the foot and wisteria began to climb across its sides.

That winter, the Architectural Design Institute played host to the annual architectural conference to which several scholars and specialists from different parts of the country were invited. Because there weren't a lot of participants, the conference was held in the ground floor meeting room of the Design Institute. No sooner had the experts entered the gate than their attention was attracted by the boundary wall. They looked it up and down, full of praise. Once the conference had got under way, the wall became the topic of conversation. They said the boundary wall solved one of the major problems of city construction! Today's city architecture was too monotonous. Everything was constructed on a standard matchbox design, unchanging and unornamented, totally lacking our own unique traditional flavour. There were also places which blindly went back to the ways of the ancients, building curving eaves with upswept corners, carved rafters and painted crossbeams with the result that hotels turned out like temple halls. The good thing about this wall was its traditional style. Yet it was not a blind restoration of the classic but done with practical economy. It also harmonized with the building itself. They hoped that comrades would carefully think things over and come to a scholarly conclusion.

Participants from the Design Institute were all pleasantly surprised. They had never imagined a golden phoenix would appear out of their hen's nest!

Director Wu pondered, "This is all because the guiding thought was clear and unequivocal. From the start I made explicit demands, at the same time rousing the masses to comprehensive discussion. . . ."

Zhu Zhou was also pondering, "Too true, the practical value of the boundary wall can't be overlooked. Right from the start I maintained that it must be taller, more secure. . . ."

Huang Daquan was quite simply delighted with himself. "If it hadn't been for me arguing for what I knew was right, who knows what unearthly shape the wall would have gone up in. Architects just can't afford to forget their origins. Our ancestors understood the magical effects of boundary walls long ago. They had scores of names for them, let alone. . . ." Huang Daquan considered this speech should be written into the opening paragraph of the summary; it would do as a foreword.

He Rujin had suffered momentary unhappiness, but

then immediately felt his contribution had really been enormous. If he hadn't insisted on economy, Ma Erli would never have gone looking for old bricks and tiles and would never have found the glazed blocks. Without the glazed blocks the wall would have been nothing out of the ordinary.

Ma Erli didn't take part in the conference; he just busied himself rushing in and out of the room arranging tables and chairs and bringing tea and water. He'd taken into consideration the fact that the room would be very cold and from somewhere or other had produced four glowing charcoal braziers. With one placed in each corner, the room immediately became as warm as springtime. Everyone felt cosy and relaxed. . . .

Translated by Rosie A. Roberts

The Gourmet

A Word About Eating

THE word gourmet is pleasing to the ear, even more so to the eye. If you explain it in simple everyday language, however, it's not so appealing: A gourmet is a person who is totally devoted to eating.

That a person who devotes himself solely to eating should be given a special name such as gourmet was something I'd never expected. But then the things you expect never happen and the unexpected often takes place right in front of your nose. It so happened a certain person who liked eating more than anything else haunted me like a spectre for forty years. I despised and loathed him. I opposed him too but in the end I turned out to have no special skills of any kind while he became known as a gourmet for his refined tastes.

I should first and foremost make it clear that I am not on the whole opposed to eating; if I had been then I would have died soon after I was born. No, that's not what I mean. Hard work and frugality are a national tradition while gluttony has always been criticized. As a child, my mother taught me that greediness was bad and would scold me by saying, "You greedy guts, you're a little good-for-nothing." And children would tease one another by poking fingers in your cheek and saying,

"Shame on you, greedy, shame." Bashful girls would never dare eat fritters or buns on the street. Growing up in this kind of environment, I always looked down on people who were too fond of good food, even more so after meeting Zhu Ziye, who'd been a glutton since childhood. After that, people who indulged themselves in eating made my stomach turn even more.

Zhu was a capitalist, a property owner who owned almost all the houses in my lane. He didn't need much skill to exploit anyone; all he had to do was say three words, "Collect the rent". He didn't need to say it in fact, since his agent would do it for him. He didn't even know how many houses he had and where they were. His father was a shrewd property dealer who'd opened an agency in Shanghai and bought a lot of houses in Suzhou. A bomb had fallen on his Shanghai home at the start of the War of Resistance Against Japan and there had only been one survivor in the whole family — Zhu, who'd been at a wedding banquet at his grandmother's in Suzhou. His liking for food had saved his life; without it he'd have died.

He was almost thirty when I met him. Don't think that all gluttons are fat; that's not so, he was as thin as a willow twig. Perhaps his thinness and a feeling that he'd never quite had enough was the reason for his gluttony. A truly tubby type wouldn't dare to eat so much. Gluttons take care of their mouths, not their appearance. Though Zhu had enough money to look after both his mouth and his looks, he had no interest in clothes at all. All year round he'd wear long gowns bought in second-hand stores. He put them on as soon as he bought them and left the dirty ones in public bathhouses. People said he was married, but he had neither children nor a woman. He'd been seen once riding in a pedicab with a pretty woman at Huqiu Hill, but people later learned that she'd been unable to get a cab, had shared one with him and he'd boorishly made her pay half the fare.

His home in Shanghai bombed, he lived by himself in Suzhou in a western-style house. It had been built in the twenties and had screen doors and windows, carpeted floors and a proper bathroom. On one balcony were two large tanks for storing water pumped up from a well. This two-storeyed building sat behind a big courtyard, in the front of which was a row of six rooms used as a gatehouse, kitchen, storage room, pantry and servants' quarters.

My maternal aunt and Zhu's paternal aunt were cousins, so when my father died a few years after the war broke out, my mother and I moved into one of the six rooms. We lived rent free but had two duties: one was to be Zhu's gatekeeper and the other was to help with the housework. They were both pretty light tasks since Zhu went out early every morning and came back late every night. He had a house but not much housework and never asked my mother to do anything. He found it a nuisance when she offered to wash his sheets or dust and air the rooms for him. He thought this entirely unnecessary. To him a home was merely a bed after over-indulgence, and the minute his head touched the pillow he'd start snoring.

Zhu got up very early and never overslept because his stomach worked like an alarm clock. As soon as he opened his eyes, the first thing that occurred to him was to go to Zhu Hongxing's to eat the first batch of noodles.

Zhu Hongxing's was well-known for its noodles. If, for instance, you sat at a table and called out, "Hey (you didn't say comrade then), give me a bowl of such-and-such noodles." The waiter would pause a minute and then sing, "One bowl of noodles coming up." The reason he waited was to see what other specifications people had for the noodles — how they were to be cooked, how much broth, how much leek, oil, or vegetables and pork were to go on top or whether or not you wanted to "cross the bridge", meaning the vegetables and pork were served as a side dish instead of in the same bowl as the noodles. This you ate by adding it to the noodles yourself. If it was Zhu at the table, the waiter would warble, "Yes sir, one bowl of lightly cooked shrimp noodles, a lot of broth and leeks, a large portion of vegetables and pork and cross the bridge."

This concoction, complicated enough in itself, was less important to Zhu than that the noodles were from the first batch. All the noodles were boiled in the same pot and since the water gradually thickened up the later noodles were never as good as the first. If he got those, Zhu would be unhappy all day, feeling all the time that something was wrong. Consequently, unlike Oblomov he couldn't sleep in but had to get up before daybreak, quickly wash his face and then get there in time for the very first batch. As with other art forms, the art of eating depended on how well one was in command of time and place.

As Zhu emerged rubbing his eyes, his rickshaw puller, A'er, would be waiting for him at the gate. Zhu would climb in ostentatiously, ring the bell with his foot and go off to Zhu Hongxing's. After that, he'd go on to a teahouse in Changmenshi Road.

There were teahouses everywhere in Suzhou and Zhu patronized this particular one because of its high standards. It was a large establishment with a few private rooms furnished with rosewood tables and rattan chairs. They made their tea with leaves straight from the Dongting Hills and rainwater boiled in an earthenware pot over a pine branch fire. Eating and drinking are an integral whole, and all gourmets like good tea.

After Zhu had settled himself down in the teahouse, his dining companions would drift in. Gourmets only ever eat alone at breakfast. Otherwise, they must have between four and eight people, since Suzhou cuisine comprises a whole set of dishes: cold ones first, hot stir-fried ones next, then sweet dishes, then further specialities, then pastries and dumplings and finally a big bowl of soup. One person cannot manage the whole array and one dish does not provide an adequate sense of Suzhou cuisine. Therefore gourmets must move in groups. Zhu and his friends would first meet at a teahouse to reflect on the delicious food they'd consumed the previous day. The conversation would then turn to the venue of the next meal. If they were fed up with the restaurants nearby, they would go to a distant one by rickshaw or carriage. . . . Unfortunately I cannot describe in detail all the delicacies of Suzhou and its environs. I'm afraid that it would make even more people hold their conferences here. It's hard to gauge the side effects of a story.

What Concerned Me

I wouldn't have loathed Zhu quite so much if he'd had nothing to do with me. He could have been a gourmet,

I could have been a poor student, and we could have co-existed in peace. But so far I've described only his breakfast and lunch; he hasn't had his supper yet.

When Zhu had finished lunch, he would go to the bathhouse. This wasn't so much to take a bath as to find a comfortable place to digest his rich meal. As they say, you get listless if you're hungry and lazy when full. His stomach full, Zhu would dazedly make his way to his rickshaw, basking in contentment, in a comfortable, languorous fairyland. He would sway back and forth in A'er's rickshaw, speeding to the bathhouse as if making an emergency visit to the hospital.

All he had to do at the bathhouse was reach out and lift the door curtain and the counter attendant would shout, "Manager Zhu is here." God knows how he'd become "manager", since property owners were usually addressed as "master". But that respectful title was no longer fashionable, had no exotic flavour. What's more, there were big masters and little ones. Small shop owners could be called master too. But managers were different; they worked in foreign enterprises or big companies, did big business and were never stingy with tips. As soon as his arrival was announced, two attendants would rush over. One on either side, they'd conduct him to a first-class room, similar to the ones you get in hotels today. It had two beds, an enamel bathtub, a wash basin and a shower. The only difference was that it was smaller and had no air-conditioning. In winter it was heated by steam from the bathhouse and in summer cooled by a fan which rotated incessantly overhead.

Like an invalid, Zhu let everything be done for him. Tea was served, his bath water run, even his shoes were removed for him. He didn't want to do anything but concentrate on his stomach. Eating was a pleasure and digestion had its appeal too; you had to experience the thing fully and mustn't be distracted by externals. The best method of concentration was to soak in warm water and think about nothing, just experience the slow movements of the stomach, thereby producing an indescribable sense of well-being. This had as much beauty as tasting exquisite food, although one could not replace the other. Inert, his eyes half-closed, he soaked drowsily for half an hour until the masseur arrived with a large board. He drew Zhu out of the tub, placed the board on top and made Zhu lie on it face downwards. Massage is a passive exercise. Strolling after lunch is also healthy but those who do it must move their legs. All anyone being massaged has to do is relax and allow their limbs to be rubbed, their body turned over, and then be helped to sit up and lie down again. The same results are arrived at without using a single ounce of energy. A true gourmet must know how to digest his food, otherwise his stomach might threaten to stop working and this would be very dangerous.

This period of exercise wasn't that long, usually not more than half an hour. Afterwards he moved over to a couch to have his limbs kneaded and pounded. This was the final stage and possibly had a soporific effect, for he soon dozed off to the light, rhythmic pounding. During his minimum three hours' sleep his stomach would evacuate its food, making room for the next meal.

I finished school before he woke up. As soon as I put down my satchel, my mother would say, "It's still Yuan Dachang Inn today; go quickly."

This made sense only to me, since I knew that Zhu still had one more meal to devour.

Zhu's supper was something special too. Just as in literature volume two must never be too similar to volume one, so he went not to a noodle place or a restaurant but to a tavern. At lunch time Zhu and his friends savoured each dish and didn't take strong alcohol for fear that it might numb their palates, making them incapable of differentiating subtleties. At supper time they could drink to their hearts' content and then have a good sleep afterwards with no fear of insomnia. So they had to go to an inn or a tavern.

Suzhou taverns served alcohol but no food apart from snacks such as dried beancurd, peanuts, fried broad beans and peppery cabbage. That was all right enough for gentlemen but not for gourmets, who were richer than gentlemen. They must have food to go with the superior wine, and a wide variety too, so they turned to another field — appetizers.

One didn't get such things in just one part of Suzhou; they were scattered all over the place in little streets, at bridgeheads and crossroads. Some were sold in shops, some in stalls, some by small vendors. No one waiter could get them all; you had to send an errand boy out to buy them. Perhaps because of my long legs, Zhu one day asked my mother, "Your Gao Xiaoting is a clever lad; could he help me out? I'll treat him well."

My mother had no particular objection. She'd been feeling bad at living rent free with no housework to do and wanted to do something for the sake of her conscience. But I didn't like the idea of being his errand boy. How could a dignified secondary school student be the attendant of a glutton!

My mother cried. We'd been poor since my father died, reliant on my sailor brother to make ends meet. "Go, Xiaoting, we're living here free of charge, we don't even pay for electricity and water; that alone would come to what we spend on food. A single word from Manager Zhu and you could be out of school and both of us out on the street. Your father left us too soon; I beg you. . . ."

So I had to put up with it. Every evening I would wait at the tavern door with a bamboo basket. When the neon signs went on, Zhu and his friends, clean and fragrant, with ruddy cheeks and in good spirits, would arrive in a line of gleaming rickshaws, bells ringing and horns bleating, weaving their way through the pedestrians like a dragon. Zhu was always at the front, and A'er, spectacularly strong and vigorous, would remove the blanket covering Zhu's knees so that he could nimbly alight. Outside the tavern, they were greeted not by the proprietor or the waiters but by two rows of ragged, filthy beggars with their bony trembling hands outstretched. Zhu was prepared, and with a wave of his hand a small bill would fly to the beggars' leader. "Off with you," he'd say.

The beggars dispersed and I, a beggar of a different kind, would walk up to Zhu with a hungry stomach, basket in hand. This beggar was different because he knew a little about geography, about history, about freedom and equality, and because he opposed gluttony and believed in human dignity. When the beggars had scattered, leaving me at the fore, I was so ashamed and furious that I felt like throwing my basket at Zhu. But I swallowed the humiliation, took the money from his hand and, following his instructions, would go off to get roast pork from Lu's shop, game from Ma's restaurant, fish from a delicatessen, goose from an old man's house, fried beancurd from Xuanmiao Temple, and other Suzhou delicacies from famous stalls and stores.

That basket over my arm, I'd make my way through the small lanes and broad streets. There were tall buildings bursting with music, and cobbled streets brightly coloured beneath neon lights. There were dimly-lit lanes as silent as cemeteries where old women scavenged in dustbins. There were lavish feasts and there were shadowy figures queuing outside grain stores, numbers chalked on their backs, waiting for the following morning's rice ration. A family holding a wedding reception would take up all the tables in the Pine and Crane Restaurant, filling Guanqian Street with carriages, pedicabs and rickshaws. The bride would wear a long gown and a veil while the guests would be in western-style suits and leather shoes. But in the corridors of the Xuanmiao Temple people who might not see tomorrow huddled together beneath ragged sacks.

> Behind the scarlet gates meat and wine rot
> On the road lie men frozen to death.

These famous lines kept coming back to me.

Zhu was generous with me, often shoving change into my pocket, with the words "Keep it," as if to a beggar.

I would stand woodenly, humiliated to the core.

"Take it and buy some meat for your grandmother."

Insult was overcome by hardship. I had been brought up by my grandmother, who was already in her late seventies, toothless, absent-minded and partially paralysed. But she had a good appetite and wanted to have meat every day, particularly roast pork cooked with fermented beancurd from Lu's shop, so well cooked that it melted in your mouth. She had no idea about prices and inflation; to her everything was still in copper coins and silver dollars. She suspected that my mother begrudged the money my brother sent home to get her pork. She accused her of mistreating her and often nagged her bitterly and at length. My mother's explanations fell on deaf ears and she wept silently, her tears falling into the ration rice as she picked the sand and gravel out of it. Those tears broke my heart.

The meat I bought with Zhu's change moved my grandmother greatly and she would stroke my hair with a quivering hand and say, "You're a good filial boy, I didn't bring you up for nothing. . . ."

When she talked like that I would almost break down and start sobbing, but instead I held back and squatted beside her bed. Why not let her derive some consolation from my insult money?

"In heaven there is paradise, on earth Suzhou and Hangzhou." I don't know who invented the saying, nor why they put Suzhou before Hangzhou. It's said to be because Hangzhou became a capital only in the Southern Song dynasty while Suzhou was prosperous several hundred years earlier during the Tang. In the last hundred years, as Shanghai became infested with foreign adventurers and ambitious businessmen, those with some foresight all bought property and owned a home in Suzhou. Since it wasn't a political and economic centre, Suzhou had much less official rivalry and was less of an investment risk. It wasn't a strategic military location either. For the last two thousand three hundred years, no war had ever started in Suzhou. It had good weather, rich resources and beautiful scenery. Through the centuries, landlords and officials, rich merchants, butchers who'd put down their knives, scholars who'd failed to move up in the world and ageing courtesans all retreated to Suzhou to pass their remaining years. This concentration of pleasure-seekers made Suzhou a city with the best gardens in the world and the most refined culinary arts. However, scenery doesn't fill the stomach and loses its appeal after a while, whereas three meals a day are indispensable. The real reason for Suzhou being ranked above Hangzhou was perhaps because of its superior food. This Suzhou pride seemed a kind of crime and injustice to me. I wondered if there was a "paradise" in hell, since there was certainly a hell in "paradise" and most people seemed to be poised on its periphery. To be honest, I didn't start becoming a believer in communism by reading *Das Kapital* and the *Communist Manifesto.* I was probably spurred on to it by Zhu and his like, who made me realize that all extravagantly elaborated "isms" were futile and only communism could solve the problems. Zhu could hardly have assumed such important airs if his property had been confiscated.

I softly sang a song which was popular in Beiping:

> On the other side of the mountain,
> Rich and poor are all the same.
> The rich must work to get food,
> No one slaves for them.

A simple song, easy enough to sing, but it helped me understand the world and to know which road to take. My future lay on the other side of that mountain.

In the winter of 1948, I decided to go to the liberated areas. I'd read *Iron Stream* and *Débâcle* and knew how hard revolution was, so I was feeling quite solemn and heroic, prepared to die on the battlefield.

I was going to fight for Suzhou. That beautiful, suffering city was sending me into battle. Before my departure, I went to the top of Huqiu Hill to bid farewell to Suzhou. That evening I took my insult money and went to buy food for Zhu and some roast pork for my grandmother for the last time. Three days after she discovered her beloved grandson had disappeared from home she died of grief.

How profoundly one remembers what happens in one's youth! I erased from my memory the persecution, the humiliations, the insults of the "cultural revolution" as though it were all some fleeting, inconsequential game. But leaving my home and family over thirty years ago is carefully stored away in my memory. Perhaps I prefer to remember honour and forget injury, but why can't I erase the outrages of thirty to forty years ago from my mind? Every time I see films of wounded soldiers struggling to stand up, raising their rifles to charge the enemy, shouting slogans of revenge, my heart aches and tears come to my eyes. Although repeating the same scenes over and over again is boring, I forbid my children to say so and scold them when they do.

A Happy Misunderstanding

I didn't realize I'd get to the liberated area too late, that the gun smoke would already have disappeared, the sound of gunfire already have died away. The soldiers and civilians were at the height of their celebrations, preparing to fight their way across the Yangtse River. Students on their way to the liberated areas were stopped halfway and sent off with the army to work in the cities once they had been taken over. Since I came from Suzhou, knew the layout of the city and understood its beautiful but difficult dialect, I was naturally sent back there. At least I could take people around. No one cared about what they would do in Suzhou — if we'd brought up the question of our futures, our vocation, wages and accommodation the way young people do today, we'd have been regarded as petty-bourgeois elements sent by the Kuomintang. Revolution was revolution and whatever you did was all right. But the officer in charge of assigning jobs wasn't careless about it and he wanted to make sure people were given work to suit their skills and interests. As a result a cheerful meeting ensued.

He summoned twenty or so students to a temple and made us sit on either side of a table in the middle of the hall. On it were papers, pens and our files.

He was an educated man who had graduated from the Department of Mechanical Engineering at Jiaotong University and knew us students quite well. "Now, I'll assign you your jobs and will do my best to see that they fit in with your skills and wishes," he began. "I hope you'll think a little before answering my questions. Once I've assigned you your jobs, you must follow instructions."

But this solemn atmosphere was destroyed by a former classmate of mine nicknamed Bighead Ding. Actually his head wasn't really bigger than normal, but his extensive knowledge of astronomy, geography, history and philosophy made it seem so. He was the first to be called.

"What would you like to do?"

"Anything," he shot back.

The man rolled his eyes upwards. "What is 'anything'? Be a little more specific."

"More specifically . . . anything."

Everyone burst out laughing. "He's a jack-of-all-trades, he can do anything."

The man laughed too and leafed through his file. "Where shall I send a jack-of-all-trades? . . . Can you tell me what you're most interested in?"

"Reading."

"Why didn't you say so before? Go to the Xinhua Bookstore."

That one sentence decided Ding's life. He later became the manager of a Xinhua Bookstore, and he was a manager who knew his job.

The second person called was a girl, a beautiful Suzhou girl, attractive in her Lenin-style cotton suit and army cap.

After one look at her, the man asked, "Can you sing?"

"Yes."

"Will you sing something from the *White-haired Girl*?"

"The north wind blows. . . ." In those days no one was too shy to sing since we sang every day.

"Good, you work in the cultural troupe."

She didn't do too badly either. Before the "cultural revolution" she was a famous folk singer. You don't hear of her these days; she's probably teaching singing somewhere.

When my turn came, I made a mess of things. I seemed to like everything except gluttony. I didn't have any particular skills and couldn't even sing properly.

The man asked impatiently, "You don't know anything at all?"

"Yes, I do, I know how to buy special foods for people, and I know all the eating places in Suzhou."

"Right, go to the commercial department. Suzhou is known for its food."

"No, no, please, I hate eating."

"You hate eating? All right. I'll tell the cook to starve you for three days. Then we'll discuss it again. Next. . . ."

Alas, my future was settled amidst general mirth. But I wasn't depressed, nor would I think of disobeying orders! Yangtse River was surging angrily, the people on its south bank were suffering. We had to rescue them from the abyss of misery and overthrow the old society where people were cruelly exploited. The life-style of parasites like Zhu Ziye had to come to an end. Well, it's beyond your control now, Zhu. We won't let you starve, but you will have to cook your own meals. A'er won't be pulling you around in a rickshaw. You've got legs, you can walk.

I returned to Suzhou and went back to live in the rooms in front of Zhu's house. Zhu treated me with respect: he addressed me as comrade, and I called him manager; he offered me expensive cigarettes, and I declined by producing my own cheaper ones. Don't pull that one on me, I thought. Just after Liberation Zhu was timid, afraid that the Party would put him in prison. Prison food would be hard to swallow.

After a while he was reassured, for during the movements to stamp out prostitution and opium, to struggle against local despots, suppress counter-revolutionaries and so on he was never touched. He was no opium addict, nor did he have an eye for prostitutes. Apart from being a glutton he hadn't really done anything. He would often give me the thumbs-up and say, "The Communist Party is good, getting rid of all the robbers, thieves, ruffians, vagabonds, gambling and opium dens. It's a lot better, a lot more stable."

So Zhu was not treated badly and kept right on eating, still riding A'er's rickshaw to restaurants and teahouses, and he still had someone to buy delicacies for him.

Those days I was up to my neck in work from morning till night without even Sundays off. When movements were in full swing I'd sleep in the office. But Zhu was even busier, leaving home before I got up and returning after I was asleep. Every time he got back he would step on the rickshaw bell, making a gong-like noise deep in the night. Sometimes he didn't come back and on summer nights, sated, would sleep in the pavilion in the cool, fragrant park. He gradually gained weight, growing a small paunch. My mother told him, "You're putting on weight, Manager Zhu; people in their forties tend to do that." "It's because I have an easy life," he said. "Now I don't have to worry about thieves and villains. Despite all the money I had, life in the past was hard. I had to remember to give people gifts on their birthdays and on festivals too or they'd beat me up or throw dirt at the rickshaw. We didn't get any peace in the restaurants either. One time, a man walked in while we were eating and told us to move. I didn't know who he was and argued with him, but it turned out I upset some gangster boss who had me beaten up and demanded four ounces of gold as an apology from me. You don't get that kind any more; they're either in prison, gone over to the Kuomintang or hiding at home. The restaurants are less crowded and cheaper. I can snooze in the park after a good meal and don't have to worry about pickpockets." He patted his belly. "So I'm getting fat."

I blinked in astonishment listening to him. I'd never expected that revolution meant liberation for him too.

Wakened by his rickshaw bell late at night, I was annoyed that Suzhou was still paradise for people like him. When the labouring masses won their liberation, these parasites benefited too. I couldn't budge Zhu, but now I had the right to publicly preach communism, so I decided to start with A'er, his rickshaw puller.

A'er lived at the lane entrance, just next to the public well. He was about my age, but taller, stronger and better looking. When we were little, we often played together and he would always be the one to climb up on the roof if our ball got thrown up there. His father was a rickshaw puller too and came from north of the Yangtse River. When he could no longer work, his son took over. He took Zhu out three times a day and took other customers the rest of the time. He had a good rickshaw with a leather canopy, a horn, a foot bell and a blanket to cover customers' knees in spring and winter. A smart rickshaw and a handsome puller attracted a lot of business, especially from pretty artists who were story-tellers or ballad singers, attractively dressed girls with *pipas* under their arms. They felt they had to hire his rickshaw. As A'er wove through the noisy streets, horn bleating and bell ringing, all the pedestrians stared. When they got to the theatre, instead of slowing down he would brake in two steps with his feet firmly gripping the ground and his body leaning backwards, arms pressing the handles tightly, stopping smoothly like a Shanghai limousine. Holding the *pipa*, the actress would get off, wiggling her bottom, looking this way and that before disappearing behind a beaded curtain. What kind of impression would she make if she'd come in a broken-down rickshaw pulled by a hunchbacked old man?

Although A'er was a rickshaw puller, for the abovementioned reasons he had a reasonably good life. When I went over to talk to him he and his family were having supper. The table was laid with a couple of dishes and good rice. His father was sipping wine and had a side dish of goose. I made a little small talk and then came right to the point.

"What do you think, A'er, now that we're liberated?"

An outspoken sort of person, A'er answered, "Things are good, we're no longer kicked around and beaten and the customers always pay their fares."

I snorted. "Is that all? The working class are the masters of this country now; we do not slave for others."

"I haven't been slaving."

"Are you sure? What do you do?"

"Pull a rickshaw."

"Right. Down the centuries all vehicles have been drawn by animals except for trains and cars."

"What about a flat cart?"

"That . . . that's for goods, not passengers. People

have legs, they're not ill or crippled. Why should somebody sit legs crossed on a rickshaw while you run in front of him like an animal? Do you call that equality? Do you call that being a master? And what about humanism?"

"Well, you've got a point there." A'er drew in his breath.

His father sighed, "We can't do otherwise; that's what they pay us for."

"Money. . . ." I drawled contemptuously. "Do you know where people like Zhu got their money from? They exploited the labouring people and then gave you pennies to make you slave for them."

A'er frowned. "That man is quite fussy. He always wants me to go fast and doesn't like being jostled."

I seized this opportunity to tell him what the future would be like when the working people became the real masters of the country.

His interest was aroused. "That'd be something to work for. Dad, let's stop pulling rickshaws, you've been a slave all your life." A'er, I knew, wanted to be a car driver, the highest goal for all young rickshaw pullers at the time.

His father lifted his glass. "Finish your supper and go to bed early; you've got to take Zhu to the noodle place in the morning." I'd wasted my breath on him. Well, I'd forget about this conservative old man.

I invited A'er to my place to talk to him more. His consciousness raised, he decided to disobey his father and find another job. I spurred him on. "Good for you. You've taken an important step. The best thing would be for you to go to a factory and be an industrial worker."

A few days later, a despondent A'er came to see me. "I've applied to a lot of places but I can't even get into a restaurant, never mind a factory."

"Don't lose heart, you must hold out at all costs."

"I haven't lost heart, but I'm hungry."

I was worried too. "That's a big problem. We'd better get something sorted out for you."

I gave him some money and went off to the civil service bureau to look up a friend who'd come back to Suzhou the same time I did.

"That's a bit unthinking," he said. "The factory owners are talking about withdrawing their capital and it's difficult to keep the factories open, so how can people expect to get jobs there?"

"Okay, I made a mistake, but we can't let him down; think of something."

He thought for a bit. "Well, at the moment I'm registering jobless people to do some work to earn their keep instead of just getting relief."

The work was dredging the small canals in Suzhou, strenuous but useful. The old society had left us with a lot of scum, so we had to clean the canal water and make this Venice of the East live up to its name. Making this paradise more beautiful was one aspect of revolution.

When A'er heard that this was also revolutionary work, he willingly went every day to dredge the canals and carry stones. It was much harder than pulling a rickshaw and he got only three catties of rice a day.

To make ends meet, A'er's father set up a little stall selling onions and ginger. He didn't do badly since he was next to the public well. People often remembered they hadn't got any onions or ginger only while they were washing their vegetables. But the wine and goose disappeared from his table. Every time he saw me the old man turned away angrily. I felt rather apologetic and thought to myself, "Don't be mad at me, uncle, some day you'll be able to drink vodka." His anger spurred me on. Every night, when I dragged my way past his door in the deserted lane, I'd think, "I haven't let you down, uncle. I'm not afraid of hard work or fatigue; your A'er and I are fighting for tomorrow."

My mother was very angry with me about A'er. "You ungrateful brat, what did Manager Zhu do to us? It's none of your business if he wants to spend money riding in a rickshaw. Now, A'er can't support his family and Manager Zhu has to hail a rickshaw when he wants to go out and sometimes gets caught in the rain."

I decided not to argue with her; she'd suffered enough in the old society. Now that life was better I didn't want her to be upset. Besides, we just saw things differently. She still believed in the old feudal virtues, in loyalty to one's master like servants in classical operas. But it did keep me from working on the man who ran errands for Zhu. He was so old he wouldn't even be able to carry stones like A'er if he lost his job with Zhu.

Zhu suspected I was behind all of this and no longer addressed me as Comrade Gao or offered me cigarettes. If we bumped into one another, he would lower his head and keep on walking. Without seeing his eyes I couldn't tell if he bore a grudge against me or just wanted to avoid me. He always carried a pair of galoshes and an umbrella, for he went out so early in the morning it was difficult to tell what kind of a day it was going to be. He didn't want to be drenched in case he couldn't find a rickshaw. I was secretly pleased. "You'll have to earn your own living sooner or later, Zhu. You might as well start practising now."

The Attack Begins

Perhaps it was something the job-assignment fellow wrote on my file, for all my later jobs were to do with food. During the nationalization of private enterprise I was sent to a private restaurant to be manager since there weren't enough state representatives.

Before Liberation I'd never set foot in the place. I'd just watched well-dressed people go in and out while the beggars crowded around the gate and looked at the delicious food in the display windows. After reading Andersen's *The Little Match Girl*, I always felt that the girl had probably died outside this very restaurant. I'd get there on snowy winter mornings and suddenly feel apprehensive, afraid she'd be lying there dead with her matches scattered all over the ground.

I hated to see arrogant and wasteful behaviour in the restaurant. About one third of the food was usually left uneaten. If I let that continue, what kind of a revolution was I making?

I first of all got the restaurant employees to discuss the kind of people we had been serving. What proportion of them were workers or peasants, and what proportion were landlords or capitalists. This was meant to stir them up because they all knew that peasants never dared set foot in our restaurant; they were scared away by its appearance and cost. One meal cost as much as several bags of rice. They preferred eating at stalls in the Xuanmiao Temple where the food was good and cheap. Workers wouldn't come either except on very special occasions. But they all knew Zhu Ziye's likes and dislikes. Each waiter could recite a long list of regular customers, not one of whom came from the proletariat. During the time when private enterprise was being reformed, the capitalists were very unhappy. For some of them it was the end of this world and they'd often come to the restaurant to get drunk. They'd order a lot of famous Suzhou dishes and toss back one glass of alcohol after another, then tipsily declare, "Eat up, friends, we'll eat our way through their tractor screws." This was a way of attacking socialism, for in those days we looked upon tractors as a symbol of socialism. Socialist agriculture meant big state farms with lots of tractors like those in the Soviet Union.

I took this material, added to it my knowledge about the behaviour, past and present, of Zhu and his friends and wrote a long report, explaining my intention of making changes in the restaurant. It was animated and sincere and an obvious declaration against excessive consumption. My superiors were very pleased and gave permission for me to try out my ideas in my restaurant first and then see about introducing them in other ones.

I set to work. First I took down the neon lights at the door and the coloured lights in the windows. It seemed to me these sorts of lights represented dissipation and luxury and were the cause of dissolution. The old society of lavish display would never be resurrected, so why should we be left with its nauseating remnants?

The inside had to be changed too. We mustn't frighten off workers and peasants. The restaurant should be simply furnished and have plenty of room.

Why should people eat in small private rooms? They could eat in public with money they'd earned from their labour. Only blood-suckers wanted to eat in hiding. With the partitions knocked down we'd have a lot more room for ordinary labourers to dine in.

The service needed reforming too. The attendants weren't old-time waiters, they were working class. They didn't have to bow and smile, tagging after customers, wiping the tables and chairs with cloths they carried on their shoulders like people in Beijing operas. We were all comrades; why should they be a lower class, why should there be such hypocrisy? And people could fetch their own chopsticks, saucers and cups and whatever else they wanted, just as if they were at home. Who apart from masters didn't set their own tables at home?

These first three reforms the staff approved of and accepted as having a revolutionary flavour. But when I got to reforming the most important thing, the menu, things weren't so easy. Deep-fried fish, snowy chicken balls, crab meat and cabbage hearts ... were all so aristocratic, who could afford them? An ordinary dish and an ordinary soup at 50 cents each were enough for one person. I had no objection to some people wanting something better, people had to have a little variety. In the revolutionary army we would often get special treats such as a bowl of stewed pork. Anyway if what I suggested was too simple, we could have something like cabbage and shredded meat, garlic and liver, steamed fish or lion's head meat balls with green vegetables. That would be enough. No working class household ate like that every day.

Objections were raised, all of them from the older employees.

A waiter named Zhang took the lead. Grinning, he began, "Heavens, is our famous restaurant going to be turned into a little cafe? Why don't you do a more thorough job, Manager Gao? Give each of us two boards and let us set up stalls at the railway station."

I raised my eyebrows. "You can say what you think, comrade, but don't make fun. You're talking about revolutionary work, not joking with customers now," I cautioned him.

"All right, I've no objection. At least we won't have as much work to do," Zhang conceded.

The accountant chipped in, "I could be wrong, Manager Gao, but I'm a bit worried that we might not earn enough money." He spoke hesitantly since he'd been got at in past political movements for being a relative of the restaurant's former owner.

"I've thought about that too, but a socialist enterprise should serve the people instead of just earning money like the capitalists."

"Yes, yes, you're right." He was convinced.

But the celebrated chefs refused to be persuaded. These days they would be ranked among the top chefs and could have written books and gone abroad to demonstrate their skills. But back then no one had any particular respect for them, nor did they have any for laymen like me. Especially Yang Zhongbao, who acted as though I'd been flaying him alive.

"So that means we'll just be serving ordinary food, the kind people eat at home," he said.

"What's wrong with that?"

"Why bother going to a restaurant when you can get the same thing at home?"

"People don't cook when they come to Suzhou on business," I reasoned.

"Then they want to try the best food we can offer, and that isn't lion's head meat balls."

"That depends on what kind of people they are."

"All kinds, including cadres like you."

"I get 50 cents a day expenses when I travel on business. If I spend that all on one meal I've still got two meals to pay for." I kept up the struggle.

"Not everyone is like you. People spend their own money too."

"How much have they got? Some of them embezzle public money just because they want to eat good food when they go out," I said, trying another tactic.

"What if you get taken out to dinner?"

"Why should you accept? A lot of people have been corrupted by capitalists through accepting invitations. A lot of evil deals have probably been worked out right in our private rooms."

"What about weddings?"

"Even less reason to be extravagant. Buy some sweets and have a party, that's what the government employees do."

Yang flared up. "You're talking like a layman, Manager Gao. Government offices are different from restaurants. Why don't you transfer me to a government office to be a canteen cook? I'll gladly go."

I glared at him, holding back what was on the tip of my tongue. I couldn't lose my temper with an old chef who'd worked longer than I'd lived, who had always been a member of the proletariat while I was an ex-student who belonged to the petty-bourgeoisie, something which couldn't be changed no matter how revolutionary I was now. At any rate, they had reason to object since their skills wouldn't be any use. Cabbage and shredded meat didn't require any high degree of skill; even I could do that. . . . It would be a pity if their talents went to waste. It would be better for him to go and cook for a foreign affairs department rather than in a mass canteen.

The room fell silent.

I turned to the younger ones, having discovered that the best way to save a situation was to stir them up a little. Even if they went too far it could still be put right later on.

"Haven't you young people got anything to say? You're in charge of this restaurant too; the future belongs to you."

They only smiled, caught between the older chefs and me. One young waiter, Bao Kunnian, still only an apprentice, spoke very convincingly:

"Our restaurant must carry out thoroughgoing reforms. We will not serve rich people any more; we must genuinely serve workers, peasants and soldiers. And our menu must show it. They can't afford crab meat and cabbage hearts. The cabbage hearts are put in that dish while they get the outer leaves. Stir-fried cubed chicken uses only chicken breast, and the claws and the heads are sold to rickshaw pullers. This is a way of looking down on the labouring people. Once when a peasant came in and ordered beancurd soup he was sent away to the Xuanmiao Temple. This was a nasty trick because the Xuanmiao Temple only serves jellied beancurd. Yet when people like Zhu Ziye turn up, the waiters and chefs get cracking right away. He gets live fish, huge prawns and the tenderest cabbage hearts."

Once Bao started, the others followed, criticizing the wastefulness in the restaurant and the way we took special care over big banquets but neglected small customers. A lot of these things I hadn't known and they infuriated me. I rapped the table, "Don't you see how badly in need of reform we are?"

Zhang hung his head in silence, possibly for having sent the peasant away. The chefs were silent too. Suzhou cuisine required a lot of superior ingredients and that made waste inevitable. And of course people like Zhu got taken good care of. Chefs relied on gourmets to spread their fame and describe the most subtle nuances of every dish.

Our policy was thus settled, thanks to Bao. He was later very active and carried out my instructions to the letter. I also gave him whatever help he needed to make progress.

He beat me half to death in the "cultural revolution", but that's another story....

I threw myself into the reforms and never got home before eleven at night. I got the interior and facade altered, put up blazing red notices and sent a write-up to the local paper entitled *Famous Restaurant Serves Inexpensive Dishes to Ordinary People.*

The first day a lot of people came — old men and women with their grandchildren, rickshaw pullers, vendors and people on business trips to Suzhou. Rickshaws, pedicabs and carriages lined the street outside. I'd seen this kind of commotion before Liberation when rich men and their wives came. While they were eating and enjoying themselves upstairs their rickshaw pullers would be out shivering in the cold. Now these same shivering people were striding into the restaurant, heads held high. Human voices and the scraping of tables and chairs rose together in a hubbub. The atmosphere was electric. The waiters brought the food quickly since the dishes were cooked in large quantities and ladled out. Going in and out, people kept to the right as though they were in traffic. The restaurant was thronged with customers.

Surprisingly, Zhu and his friends came too. Right, I wanted to see quite what they'd eat today. They read the notice outside, came in and looked around, bent down and scrutinized the dishes. Sniffing in contempt, they left, slapping each other on the back and sniggering. I was furious. "Go ahead and oppose me, sirs; that's exactly why I want to change this place."

But the reaction of the old men and women was quite different. "Before we just heard about this place but never dared come in. Today we've really seen something."

One peasant choosing his meal observed, "Whenever I came here in the past I always had to go to the kitchens through the back door to deliver vegetables. I never dared poke my head into the restaurant."

Their praise made me forget my fatigue and touched me deeply. No matter how history assessed my work during this period, I firmly believed I was whole-heartedly and selflessly engaged in working in a great cause.

Our superiors paid a visit and were very satisfied. Although things were still a little chaotic, this was considered inevitable at the outset and we were asked to summarize and relay our experience to other restaurants.

A Happy Outcome

Zhu had been driven to the wall. Although a lot of the other famous restaurants didn't really follow suit and just made do with showing a few ordinary dishes in their windows, their specialities deteriorated in quality. The same dish at the same price was cooked with much less care. As soon as he tasted the difference, Zhu would frown, shake his head and complain. But he was misjudging the situation. No one paid any particular attention to him any more, no one called him Manager Zhu. A property owner, though still rich, no longer had any clout. Waiters weren't allowed to accept tips. It was up to you whether you came in or not; the volume of business didn't affect people's salaries. Anyone taking much notice of Zhu's complaints would be labelled "a servant of the bourgeoisie". Every meal was torture for Zhu and his stomach. He never ate his fill, and looking at the food gave him indigestion. He wandered around like a lost soul, buying pastries which he'd find weren't as good as before and then leave them to go mouldy till my mother threw them away. His little paunch slowly dwindled.

One night, a tipsy Zhu pushed open my door and announced, "I . . . oppose what you stand for, Manager Gao."

The bourgeoisie was counter-attacking. "Your opposition is welcome."

"You're making a mess of Suzhou cuisine; you're unfair to Suzhou."

"That's only your opinion. I haven't made a mess of anything. I don't make the landlords and capitalists very happy to be sure, but I think I've served the people of Suzhou well."

"You. . . . You're ungrateful to me."

"That's right; that's to be expected because you belong to the bourgeoisie."

"But I've been kind to you, Xiaoting."

Zhu was tactless enough even to compliment himself for behaviour which had wounded my pride. I flared up. "I haven't made you or your friends happy, Manager Zhu. Three of them were landlords, two belonged to reactionary groups while you and two others still live on money the state gives you as compensation for your investments. Don't think you'll get that for ever."

Startled, Zhu sobered up and retreated a few steps. I declined the high-quality cigarette he quickly offered and took out one of my cheaper ones. He put the cigarette to his lips and inhaled.

"Ah, somebody bought me a chicken today somewhere outside Suzhou which was just as good as the ones I used to eat, so I ended up having a few too many. I don't even know how I got here; where's the door?" He turned to go.

"Wait."

He halted.

"Manager Zhu, I should have shown you my gratitude by warning you to change your way of living and learn to earn your own keep."

"Right, right, I'll bear that in mind."

After that, I didn't see much of him and he never came to complain again. I often asked my mother about him. She didn't know much either except that he was seldom home and his room had a mouldy smell. He must be out doing something, I thought. Eating was his permanent necessity but it couldn't be his lifelong profession.

A while later, Bao gave me a report — he always used to report things to me.

"Chef Yang has opened an underground restaurant specially for capitalists and is earning a packet every night."

"Are you sure?"

"Absolutely, I saw it with my own eyes. It's in No. 54, east of where you live. Every night a lot of these capitalists go there. Yang cooks while a seductive-looking woman collects the money."

If there was any truth in what Bao said, how could I ignore it? I made investigations, sounded Yang out and unearthed Zhu's retreat.

No. 54 was the home of a woman named Kong Pixia, the former concubine of a politician-cum-professor, and her three tenants. She was not unusual among Suzhou residents. It was said she'd been as beautiful as a goddess when young, had been taught by a famous opera singer, and had even played a part in *The Goddess Scattering Flowers*. But even a goddess loses her attraction after forty, and on the eve of Liberation her husband abandoned her and her eight-year-old daughter and fled to Hongkong.

Probably because she'd once been on stage, Kong still liked doing herself up, and her every movement and glance was intended to look beautiful. When overdone, however, it was affected and coquettish — a little strange, in fact, since there was not much left to be coquettish about.

Zhu, who had never had any interest in women, got mixed up with Kong simply because of her marvellous cooking. Kong had prepared many banquets for her husband and his friends, men from political, industrial and cultural circles who were socially a cut above Zhu. To them Zhu was nothing more than a rich man and a glutton. No true gourmet dined in restaurants all the time. None of the banquets in *A Dream of Red Mansions* were in restaurants. First-batch noodles were nothing to them. They were people who sipped tea in moonlit gardens and drank wine by balustrades overlooking streams. It was indecorous to eat roast pork that came wrapped in lotus leaves and fermented beancurd strung together with a rice stalk in noisy inns. People of taste and influence went to restaurants only when social occasions required them to and then only picked at the rich, greasy food. The pots and spatulas were not washed between cooking, so the food always had a mixed smoky taste. To them Zhu's delicacies were coarse fare indeed. What they ate belonged to another school of Suzhou cuisine, the crystallization of the highest forms of material and cultural accomplishment. Food as an art found its full expression in this kind of cooking.

Kong belonged to this school. When she'd been a celebrated concubine in social and cultural circles she sang opera, cooked and painted. For over twenty years, distinguished people gathered at her home to play mahjong and feast. She also employed a good cook, but only as her assistant.

Just when Zhu felt totally disappointed, somebody told him about Kong.

"You're kidding, my friend," he laughed. "I don't think home cooking can be so good. People don't have as many ingredients or as big a stove and pots as they do in restaurants."

"I don't know how I can prove it to you. In the past she wouldn't have given people like us a second look. I never managed to be invited to her place before Liberation.... But I hear she's come down in the world in the last few years and is hard up for money, so maybe she just might prepare a banquet for us. You two are neighbours, why don't you ask her and see?"

Zhu was desperate to find somewhere to eat so he decided to make a visit and put forward the proposal.

Before Liberation Kong would have thrown him out. But now, unlike Zhu, she had neither income nor any property compensation and had to rent parts of her house out to three families. Even with this, she still had to sell pieces of furniture and jewelry from time to time. She was also keen to practise her cooking skills and win praise the way she had in the past. All the same, she didn't give her consent right away.

"Oh Mr Zhu, who's been telling stories about me? I only used to cook to amuse myself," she said in her lilting Suzhou dialect.

Zhu took the hint and unashamedly begged her, "Please do us this favour. Anything you do would be preferable to what we could get in restaurants."

"Restaurants!" Kong drawled contemptuously, "I don't understand how you men can bear to eat restaurant food. The smell alone is enough to put you off."

Zhu was stunned. What sort of smell did she mean? Some of them had wonderful aromas, ones which really picked up your appetite. But he said, "Yes, we're vulgar people who don't know anything about food at all. Please open our eyes for us."

"Very well, I'll try to do what I can. How many will there be?"

Zhu counted, "Nine altogether."

"No, no more than seven. You can't cook good food in large portions."

"How about eight? That'll be the right number to fill a table."

"You don't know the rules, Mr Zhu. One place must be for the cook."

"I beg your pardon," he said, wondering about cooks joining the meal. But to satisfy his palate, he had to go along with the rules. He produced a wad of notes and counted out fifty yuan. This he laid on the table, intending to give a ten yuan tip.

Kong looked a little hesitant. "Goodness, what can we get with so little money?"

The determined Zhu put the rest of his money down, eighty yuan all told.

Kong hesitated for a while as if calculating something. Glancing up at him, she finally said, "All right, if it's not enough, I'll put some money in too. You're a sorry lot."

Kong spent five days making preparations. People said she had to give up her plan to include eel in the menu because the eel had to be kept alive in a special manner for a week first, but Zhu just couldn't wait that long.

I didn't go to the banquet, so I can't really tell you what they had.

Yang was there. He'd happened to run into Zhu while he was notifying his friends of the feast. One of them had fallen ill, and he had to find a replacement. "Come with me, it'll be an eye-opener for you," he told

Yang, explaining his arrangement with Kong, and expressing again his disappointment with my restaurant.

A good cook himself, Yang never thought much of other people's cooking. Moreover, all the famous chefs were men, and he doubted a woman's ability. But he'd also heard from his master that ever since the end of the Qing dynasty, high-class brothels in Suzhou had served excellent food prepared by beautiful, intelligent women as exquisitely as if they were doing embroidery. He didn't have much else to do anyway, so why shouldn't he accept the invitation and learn something? If the food wasn't as good as Zhu had described he could make fun of him and take him down a peg.

Yang was furious at the groundless accusation that he was running an underground restaurant and demanded to be transferred to a foreign affairs department. That was done quickly, so I never knew what skills Kong had displayed that evening.

Zhu's behaviour showed that it must have been a superb meal.

From then on, Zhu was seldom seen and stopped wandering about aimlessly. He never again went to the noodle place early in the morning and ate all his meals at Kong's. Soon the two of them, a rich man with a good appetite and an excellent cook and good shopper, linked up in marriage.

So Zhu finally married. A man who already had countless houses got himself a home at 45. A home is a wondrous thing; it can serve as a curb, can civilize a person. Zhu became decorous and decent, wearing smart suits with two fountain pens clipped to his breast pocket like a scholar. Kong spruced him up along the lines of her former husband.

Kong's housekeeping was as good as her cooking. After their marriage, she got Zhu to move in with her and moved her three tenants to Zhu's place. Her house had a little walled garden with trees, bamboos, rocks, a pool and bridge. They could live in seclusion and eat anything they liked. In those days, there were a lot of people who were opposed to good eating and fine clothes and who considered anyone who ate and dressed well as bourgeois. Therefore the rich had to eat behind closed doors. No one knew what they had in their stomachs. Of course people couldn't fail to notice the dressed-up Zhu and Kong when they went out shopping, arm in arm. They always drew a great deal of attention.

My mother never said anything bad about Kong, who she thought had done a good deed by reforming the errant Zhu. In fact, she often said to me, "Zhu has changed for the better; they're in love and look after each other."

I hesitated and thought to myself: Call this a change for the better? These people are evading reformation!

A Man and His Palate

I had no way of stopping Zhu from evading reformation. He kept away from my restaurant and I couldn't freeze his bank deposits. It was no use criticizing him for having a bourgeois mentality either, since he was nothing but a member of the bourgeoisie. Let him eat, provided he abided by the law, stopped claiming that Suzhou cuisine had deteriorated and didn't storm into my room to voice his complaints. Revolution didn't happen overnight.

He never came again, and even when we met by chance he would ignore me and sweep past, displaying his re-emerging paunch like a victorious rooster.

What really got me was how so many other people had the same ideas as Zhu and said that our restaurant had lost its reputation, that the service and the quality and variety of our menu had deteriorated. And more than ninety percent of these were not members of the bourgeoisie; they were cadres, workers, old men and women. Within a year, their support had turned to opposition. How quickly they had changed! I patiently explained to one old customer, "Now don't complain, granny, a year ago you wouldn't have been able to come in here."

"All right, now I'm in, and I want good food." She held out some money. "My son sent me this and told me to go out and have something really good when I felt like it. But what do you have here? I could do better than this myself."

"Then cook yourself. Home cooking's always best." A slip of the tongue, I was thinking of Kong.

She was furious. "You sound like the manager of a den of thieves. If I cook myself, what do you do? Get paid for doing nothing?"

Bao butted in, "What do you mean by a den of thieves. Are you calling a socialist enterprise that? Why, you're attacking. . . ."

I quickly stopped him. "Forget it, don't get angry, granny. If you haven't touched your food yet, you can have your money back."

When cadres criticized us I was less polite and would ask them, "Are you here on business, comrade?"

"Yes, I'm from Beijing," replied one. "I've come

specially to your restaurant for a taste of the famous Suzhou cuisine, but is this all you've got to offer?"

"This is plenty good enough, comrade, what's your daily expense allowance?"

"I'm putting in some of my own money."

"We must keep to our tradition of frugality."

"Yes, yes, thank you for your sermon. If I'd known I would have brought a sack of corn buns with me and then your restaurant wouldn't need to exist." He left in a huff.

I sighed, thinking his bourgeois ideas were too entrenched. As soon as he'd got some money he'd got all high and mighty. Well, it seemed our restaurant had some problems. With the economic development and good harvests in the past couple of years, prices were low while workers and cadres earned good wages. People with money to spend shook their heads at the ordinary food we sold. I wanted to serve ordinary people but they criticized me. Some of them spoke their minds while most, not caring to waste their breath, simply avoided us and went to other restaurants which had only pretended to make reforms. Once the campaign passed, they dropped their pretensions and displayed exquisite dishes in their windows again. They were making people spend money and their business was flourishing. We'd had our day too, at the beginning of the reforms, but we soon went downhill and would be in big trouble if it went on.

Gourmets! When you were poor you would have had these classy restaurants torn down, but as soon as you get a little money you all pile in, worried you won't get a seat, and you want high-class meals too.

The spring of 1957 was a troubled time. The restaurant employees began to write big-character posters saying what they thought of me and hung them in the corridor. Their objections to the food and the drop in business didn't upset me, but one signed "our employee" accusing me of seeking personal glory at the expense of the restaurant and its employees made me furious. The adjectives used in the poster and its tone meant it could only have been written by that scoundrel Bao! Of course I had to accept all the criticisms even if they had only the minutest grain of truth in them.

Just while I was so troubled and bewildered by all that was happening, my old schoolmate Bighead Ding, on his way to a conference in Beijing, stopped off in Suzhou to see me. It was eight years since we'd met and I was overjoyed. "You must come out to dinner, we can go to our restaurant," I said, a little surprised at myself wanting to take people out to dinner as soon as I saw them. It wasn't like me.

He shook his head. "Thanks, but I've been there and I've read the posters. Tell me what you have been doing all these years."

"What have I been doing? Well, just hold on a bit and I'll tell you all about it." I called my wife in and introduced Ding to her. "This is the Bighead Ding I've talked about so much. Ding, this is my wife."

Ding bowed. "I'm Ding Zhen, Bighead was my nickname. . . . But don't tell anybody else I'm a manager just like you."

My wife smiled, scrutinizing his head as if trying to determine whether or not it was really bigger than average.

"Don't stand there gaping! Why don't you go and buy some food?" Ding had already been to my restaurant and I didn't want to become a laughing stock by taking him to another one. I'd better ask my wife to make something at home.

During the two years we'd been married my wife hadn't cooked very much. All she could do was give him tea and cigarettes and say, "You two chat for a while. Mother has gone to a neighbourhood committee meeting. She'll get you something when she comes home."

The neighbourhood meetings were always marathons. The food market would be closed by the time she finished. "Why don't you cook something today? You can't depend on mother all the time."

"Have you forgotten?" she retorted. "You always say young people mustn't spend time on cooking if they want to get ahead. This ambitious young woman doesn't know where the oil is."

Ding burst out laughing. "I'll bet that's exactly what he said, so let him take the consequences."

"All right, then go and tell mother we have a guest and ask her to come back."

After she went out I began to unburden myself, starting right at the beginning. "You've read those posters. One of them was a personal attack by a young man. The rest were about my work. Where have I gone wrong in these reforms? You know what it was like in the old days. I have been working to eliminate that kind of wrong. Now those posters are attacking me for doing just that. But I haven't done anything wrong."

Ding fell silent, inhaling deeply on his cigarette. He was probably very troubled too.

"Well, say something! You're well read, you've been

working in a bookstore all these years. Pick up a book and give me a thump on the head. You'd better choose a hard-cover one and give me a really good whack."

Ding laughed. "That's no good, it'll spill your brains out. I would, however, like to draw your attention to a strange physiological phenomenon. It seems that the palate of the bourgeoisie is similar to that of the proletariat. The capitalists prefer shrimps to shredded meat and cabbage, and once they've tasted them, so do the proletariat. So when they've got the money they order shrimps, but you keep pushing shredded meat and cabbage at them. I'm surprised they haven't come after you with a hammer!"

I blew up. "You can't live on shrimps."

"Of course you can't; who can afford to do that?" he retorted.

"But we get so many people, you mustn't underestimate bad tendencies, comrade."

"It's you who've underestimated them. They've got money now. If one out of a hundred wants shrimps, that's enough to fill your restaurant to bursting. You keep rattling on about liberating the working people, but then you think they're not up to your expectations. People want to eat shrimp now and again and are quite happy to let you make a little profit, but this grates on you."

"It certainly does not! I don't have anything against them."

"I know you don't like that Zhu character, but what can you do about him when he shuts himself away?"

"He doesn't hide himself away entirely."

"Of course, a lot of people other than the working masses will be eating shrimp. I'll tell you: even when the landlords and capitalists have been eliminated, you'll still have hooligans and thieves among your customers, even escaped murderers."

I believed him. You needed an official letter and an ID card to get a room in a hotel, but only money to go to a restaurant. "You're right," I sighed. "But I still think frugality is one of our national virtues. Why should we place so much emphasis on food?"

"I know, and from your personal point of view it's a fine thing. I hope you'll keep on being frugal. But you're a restaurant manager and you can't bring all your personal feelings into your work. Suzhou cuisine is famous; it's something created by labouring people over a long period of time. If you destroy it history will hold you responsible."

I went cold. My schooling had taught me the importance of history. I would get nowhere if I resisted historical trends. Anyway I doubted that this cuisine was something created by labourers; it was obviously invented by people like Zhu and Kong.

On top of that, my mother shouldn't have given us such a lavish supper, five dishes and a delicious soup.

Ding was all smiles. "Look, this trend is sneaking into your home! You'd better watch out!"

Pumpkins and the Like

After Ding left, I did some careful thinking. Why did I want to get good food when an old friend turned up? Most simply, it was because I enjoyed doing it as well as showing my respect for a friend. Why didn't I do it before? When I said goodbye to him at Wuhan eight years ago I'd given him a send-off with a bowl of dumplings that cost five *fen*. He was happy and I demonstrated my affection. Why couldn't I do that instead of spending five yuan on food? Because five *fen* was a tenth of all the money I had then. Now, with my increased income, five yuan was the equivalent of five *fen* in those days. Even if Ding wouldn't have minded a bowl of dumplings, my mother and wife would have scolded me for being stingy. "You've missed Ding all these years, yet when he comes you won't spend more than five *fen*. What kind of person is that?"

Well, I had to be somebody who was consistent and didn't just follow bad tendencies. But had I noticed time passing, and life changing? To forget the past was a betrayal, yet refusal to change was also a betrayal, for it ran counter to the wishes of the people. Well, I'd forget about Zhu and let him have a good time in his cosy nest.

Just as I was about to accept these new ideas, the anti-Rightist movement started. It didn't hurt me; in fact I was almost a hero. People said I had a firm standpoint and had proved through my actions that the capitalists had been wrong in claiming that "the present was worse than the past". Still I wasn't really active enough since I had a change of heart after Ding's visit. I missed a chance of promotion.

The movement was followed by the Big Leap Forward and people were too busy to care about food that much. After that came the three years of natural disasters when people had nothing to eat. Ordinary food was a luxury; anything edible was welcome. No one particularly cared about the taste.

It was a bad time for Zhu. He'd spent his whole

life satisfying his palate rather than his stomach. Delicious tastes came from delicate foods like vegetable hearts, fish tails, egg whites, lean meat, mushrooms and ham. During the years when these were scarce even a good cook like Kong couldn't produce a tasty dish.

People are strange creatures. When there's food about their taste buds are highly sensitive; salty, delicate, savoury, sweet, hot, all can be differentiated. When there's nothing to eat, hunger takes over and three large bowls of plain rice give one an indescribable contentment and satisfaction. Zhu wasn't exempt from this law either. Hunger drove him out of his nest to roam about, not for delicacies this time but to see if there were crowds of people anywhere. He'd race over and squeeze in, try to buy sweet potatoes, turnips or peanuts at any price. More often than not, he would go home past my door empty-handed, exhausted and despondent. For the first time I saw him drop his airs; for the first time he realized that money wasn't omnipotent. He felt that he was given less rice than Kong's daughter.

"You're seeing things," Kong snapped.

"Is it me or you? My bowl is practically empty."

Kong shoved her daughter's bowl at him. "Here, take this one too; she's not your daughter anyway."

The child sobbed while husband and wife had a terrible row. After that they ate separately, with Zhu cooking his own meals. No longer were they seen arm in arm, nor did people hear her coquettishly calling him.

I was hungry too. As a restaurant manager, there were ways I could get food. In times like this, power was more effective than money. But I never cheated and would rather have died of hunger than lose my integrity. Besides, I didn't starve. Both the women in my family took good care of their charge. My mother would always urge me, "You eat first, you've got to go to work and I'm staying home. I'll eat later." I knew what "later" meant, so I stealthily put some rice back in the pot. My wife made sure that our daughter had enough to eat. She was at primary school and growing, and wanted to eat as soon as she got home from school. She'd eat as much as she was given, not like children today who have to be coaxed into eating.

My wife had never been all that strong and fell ill, her legs and face swelling up. This was a common illness in those days and could easily be cured with a chunk of pork and a chicken cooked with four ounces of rock sugar, but there was nowhere to get these.

With a heavy heart I was dragging my way past A'er's door one day when he signalled to me.

When he was dredging the river he'd proved himself a very good member of the working class by working hard and not grumbling about being paid only three catties of rice a day. The leader had a high opinion of him and transferred him to a transportation unit where he'd become chairman of their trade union. He still trusted me and listened to every word I said. Hadn't history proved that the rickshaw had been consigned to museums and that pedicabs were hardly seen? Although he hadn't become a driver, he had become the drivers' boss.

I went into his place. His father was in the courtyard. After ignoring me for a couple of years, he'd started to ask me to have a drink with him after A'er began to earn a monthly wage, got married and got his two younger brothers working too. Where the stall selling ginger and onions had been there was now a small table where he would sip a little wine every evening. But since things were taking a turn for the worse once again he'd taken his table inside. I still called him uncle, a greeting he acknowledged unsmilingly.

A'er took me aside. "How is your wife? She looked pretty bad when I saw her the other day."

"Yes, she's got dropsy."

"We sent two trucks to Zhejiang to get some bamboo but they came back with two loads of pumpkins instead. Bring a cart to the dock before dawn tomorrow and I'll give you some."

"You shouldn't do that! They're for the people in your organization; I can't take any."

"I'm not up to anything bad, I'm giving you my share. We often send trucks out to get food; I'm much better off than you."

"But. . . ."

"No more buts, do as he says," the old man cut in. "What's so special about pumpkins? I'm waiting for those big state farms and tractors and some of your vodka," he chided.

I laughed. "Don't give me a hard time, uncle. Remember how you used to ignore me when A'er was dredging the river? Then later you invited me for a drink every time you saw me. Don't be too impatient. These hard times are only temporary. The good times will come back."

He nodded and laughed. "I know, I know."

People like him who'd suffered in the old society and had a better life in the fifties never lost heart during those difficult years; they knew that retrogression only meant destruction and that hope lay ahead. They therefore patiently put up with hardships and waited for the good times to come back, though the waiting was long. I regretted that I hadn't given my customers more shrimps to increase their confidence in the future.

My mother was overjoyed and set off immediately to borrow a cart. The cart brought Zhu Ziye in its wake. He looked wary and pitiful. He wouldn't take a seat and just stood at the door looking foolish. I wondered if he had come to complain about something again.

My mother, as respectful to him as ever, made him sit down and gave him a cup of tea. "Say what you have to say, Mr Zhu. Did you have a row with your wife?"

"I haven't got that much energy! Look at me, I'm all skin and bones," he sighed, patting his sunken stomach which had protruded twice before, a barometer of his existence.

That paunch gone and his ruddy face sunken, he looked haggard and older. "Have patience, Mr Zhu. Hard times temper you," I said.

"Right, you're right." He rose hesitantly and then sat down again. Mother had gone through hardships herself and knew that Zhu had a favour to ask. Before Liberation, when she had to borrow money from Zhu, she'd gone in and out many times before she could bring herself to ask. Not wanting other people to suffer the way she did, she prompted him.

"Tell us what's on your mind; maybe we can help. Everybody has difficulties in their life."

"Pumpkins. I hear you're getting some pumpkins, can I buy some from you?"

This was a surprise. As the pumpkins were supposed to build up my wife's health, my mother was at a loss, remembering old stories of loyal servants helping their masters in distress. She turned to me. "What do you say, Xiaoting?"

The Zhu Ziye who had perched arrogantly on A'er's rickshaw and who'd dined in all manner of eating places was pitifully begging for a few pumpkins. This was enough punishment for him.

I nodded. "You can have some."

"Thank you very much, I'll pay you." He shoved his hand into his pocket, never forgetting the power of money.

He'd managed to hit the wrong note. Disgusted, I said, "I don't want money, but I do have a condition."

"What is it?" He looked worried.

"You must come along and help me cart the pumpkins. Those who don't work don't eat. You wouldn't want me to deliver them to your house, would you?"

"Of course not, I'll work. But . . . I don't know how to pull a cart. I might overturn it into the river."

He was right. "You can push while I pull," I said.

"Fine, I'll do my best."

"Good, come to the corner store at four tomorrow morning. Make sure to be there on time." A labourer must have discipline, I thought.

At 3:55 the following morning, I pulled the noisy cart through a slumbering lane.

Zhu, wrapped tightly in a raincoat, had planted himself conspicuously beneath a streetlamp. I was pleased. Manual labour could reform people; at least he'd learned to be on time.

"Good morning, Mr Zhu, I'm sorry to have kept you waiting."

"I've smoked five cigarettes already." He took off his raincoat and bent down to push the cart.

I quickly urged him to put his coat on and told him that an empty cart didn't need pushing. And I showed him how to raise the handle a little. "See? When the front is higher, the centre of gravity is at the back and you can pull the cart without too much effort. When we've loaded it, all you need to do is give me a hand when we go up and down slopes and bridges. When we're on level ground, just put one arm on the cart, press your weight down and run along beside it."

Zhu heaved a sigh of relief. So pushing carts wasn't that hard! He walked along beside me, his raincoat over his arm, looking around animatedly as if seeing the city and the street cleaners for the first time.

"What time is it, Manager Gao? It feels like midnight to me."

"Three minutes past four. Haven't you got a watch?" I wondered why he had measured the time by the number of cigarettes he had smoked.

"I had a Longines watch in my first year at university but I only wore it for three days. I didn't like having it on my wrist."

I almost burst out laughing. That Longines watch must be in his stomach now. That was the best place for it.

"How did you get to class on time then?"

"I didn't go. It was a private university where you could buy diplomas. I regret that I didn't study hard now. There're still so many new words when I read a book."

I looked at him in a new light. If he didn't push carts, at least he read. And reading was educational.

"What do you read?"

"Books about food, of course. Cookbooks. Now that food is scarce, I lie in bed at night remembering the goodies I had before and then all those exquisitely decorated dishes seem to appear right before my eyes. To tell you the truth, my memory is particularly good where food is concerned. I can remember what I had dozens of years ago from a certain chef in a particular restaurant, how it tasted and what the aftertaste was like. Don't you laugh. The aftertaste is important. Green olives are neither salty nor sweet nor crispy but they have a savoury aftertaste. Human beings are highly intelligent in creating so many good foods. They eat creatures that fly in the sky, that live on the land and in the seas and rivers. Otherwise they wouldn't exist today. Dinosaurs ate only grass. Where are they now? . . . Don't sigh. It's a pity that I didn't keep a detailed diary of all the good food I've eaten. So I read cookbooks to satisfy my craving. Slow down a bit and listen to me. I sometimes get angry with those cookbooks which are too general and don't include my favourite foods. What gets me is that they don't give any space to Suzhou cuisine but to queer things that the emperors used to eat. The hundred dishes they had every day were only for show; how many of them were good? Why did Emperor Qianlong come to the south three times? For Suzhou food of course. . . ."

I'd had enough. "Hurry up, let's go get the pumpkins." I stressed the word pumpkins to bring him back to reality.

"Right, we shouldn't overlook pumpkins; they can be made into something superb too. Your restaurant used to have a famous dish called 'watermelon bowl', or also 'watermelon chicken'. You cut the top off a medium-sized melon, take out the inside, leaving about one inch of flesh, and carve designs on the rind. Then you fill it with a well-steamed young chicken, replace the lid and steam it a minute. Serve the melon on a lotus leaf, which gives a cool green effect." After memorizing the recipe, Zhu shook his head. "Actually the chicken doesn't taste like melon and the sweet melon doesn't go with the salted chicken either, it's just to give it a pleasant cool greenness. We could invent a pumpkin bowl and fill it with steamed glutinous rice, nuts and preserved fruit. Sweet pumpkin would be just the thing for glutinous rice pudding; it would have a country flavour."

His long recital about food brought us almost to the dock. I didn't interrupt him, having no confidence in his transformation any more. People don't change their basic natures.

Landing in the Same Boat

It was beyond my wildest notions that an opponent of gluttony and a glutton would stand side by side one day. Yet in the "cultural revolution" I was labelled a capitalist roader while Zhu was called a bloodsucker. Every morning we stood in front of the neighbourhood committee with placards round our necks confessing our "crimes".

There was reason to call Zhu a "blood-sucking vampire". But I . . . maybe I was a capitalist roader. Once the years of natural disasters were over, I'd wanted to make amends for the reformation I'd carried out earlier and didn't force cabbage and shredded meat on the customers any more. Since times were changing, the higher-ups issued an order to open better restaurants selling costlier dishes in order to take a bit of currency out of circulation. It was incumbent upon famous restaurants like ours to take the lead. Those hard, hungry years had even made me, who'd never been greedy, crave good food. My mother went to the free market where prices were unbelievable. She bought a chicken and made some chicken broth for my wife. "Eat, my child," she urged her, tears in her eyes. "You've had a hard time these few years." Actually my wife had recovered a long time ago, but my daughter was very pleased and told everybody, "We had a chicken today," as if it was something terrific.

Zhu and Kong came back to my restaurant, not arm in arm but carrying a basket filled with sweets and pastry, each holding one side and smiling at one another. Fresh from the hairdresser's, they were sleek and perfumed. Money had played its part in patching up their worn-out love.

Zhu ordered two fresh hams cooked with rock sugar and soya sauce at the exorbitant price of 20 yuan apiece and put them into two food boxes to take home. Ever since our pumpkin adventure, Zhu and I would exchange greetings and a few words on the weather whenever we met. The lean years were finally over and we could get provisions again. Exhilarated, I said to him, "I'm glad to see old customers."

He was all smiles and shook my hand, but his answer was not pleasant to the ears. "I don't have any alternative. We can't get rock sugar and fresh ham otherwise. Your prices are exorbitant."

"Eh. . . . Why don't you eat them now while they're hot?"

"Because they're underdone and tasteless. We'll cook them again, then put them on top of some green vegetables on a white plate to make them look nice, smell good and taste delicious. Your cooking leaves much to be desired."

This wet blanket made me regret ever having given him the pumpkins, but I decided not to show my displeasure. The food supplies were improved in 1963 and '64; I had to give my customers more shrimps so that they would remember the good times and I wouldn't feel remorseful again. But rehabilitation was a hundred times more difficult than carrying out reformation. It was always easier to go from refinement to coarseness, strictness to carelessness, diligence to laziness and from being humble to being unreasonable. To correct these tendencies was much more difficult.

Although Bao was still a waiter, he hadn't actually worked as one since I'd declared during the reform years that waiters shouldn't be humble and obsequious. He sat commandingly, like some president at a meeting, and shouted to the customers, "Hey there, you're not to take any table you like. Fill the ones in front first. Hey, didn't you hear me? Why did you slip over to the window all by yourself?"

When customers asked him, "Could you come here, comrade?" he would demand, "You want to order? The menu's on the blackboard; read it."

"Comrade, I'd like to order a couple of your famous Suzhou dishes."

"Every famous dish has a name, and they're written on the blackboard." He wouldn't budge.

I would get complaints at almost every meal. "We've come to eat, not to be pushed around." I made apologies and called a staff meeting to look at our work, criticize each other and establish proper guidelines.

When the "cultural revolution" broke out these became my "crimes". I was accused of restoring capitalism and forcing the revolutionary masses to wait on city lords.

Bao became a leader of the revolutionary masses and headed straight for me, thinking that if you overthrew a director or a manager you could take their place. Since the director had already been overthrown by others he had to be content with overthrowing me. And he did have the qualifications to attack me: he had a clean record, had always supported the revolutionary line, and even more precious, he'd boycotted my restoration activities as early as 1963 and had been cruelly suppressed by me. That wasn't a lie, for I had criticized him in 1963. His remark about every famous dish having a name had been quoted in the newspapers and although his name wasn't mentioned he felt the pressure all the same. Therefore, his condemnation of my "crimes" had a particularly vehement tone: "It was a time when black clouds hung low over the city. I was alone and powerless and had to capitulate to his wishes. How I wanted to. . . ." He often read novels during working hours and had picked up a lot of phrases which he used as heavy bombs against me. I'd taken him as my right-hand man and had told him about my life, about things like running errands for Zhu and living in his house rent free and so on. I'd told him partly to show the injustice of the old society and partly to make conversation. Now he put it all together and denounced me.

"This unrepentant capitalist roader was bought by the capitalists when still a boy. Seeing the inevitable end of the Kuomintang he sneaked to the liberated area with ulterior motives. After Liberation he pretended to be active in order to worm his way up to usurp power and restore capitalism when the opportunity arose." His accusation, though groundless, was logical, for I had in reality gone to the liberated area on the eve of Liberation and had worked very hard and then been promoted to manager. I'd intended to alter my way of management when the opportunity arose after the bad years. You could look at a thing from lots of angles. If you made up your mind to call any animal a horse no matter what it was, then it couldn't be otherwise.

"Bao has a point. All property owners collect rent; why didn't Zhu make him pay? It's been a long time. What's their relationship?" People wondered. They weren't malicious, just curious.

Bao went to our neighbourhood committee to interrogate Zhu and try to dig up incriminating facts.

Besides being a glutton, Zhu's other weakness was his fear of pain. As soon as Bao rolled up his sleeves and pounded the table threateningly he started trembling and admitted to everything.

"Speak up, did you buy Gao Xiaoting?"

"Yes. . . . I did."

"How did you do it?"

"I gave him money."

"Where did you give it to him?"

"At the wineshop."

"How much?"

"Hundreds of thousands of dollars."

"How could you get such a large sum out of the bank?"

"I didn't need to go to the bank. It was all small notes, devalued Kuomintang money."

"You call that money too? What's the use of devalued money? Tell me about your collaboration after Liberation."

"There wasn't any. He hasn't been very polite to me."

"Rubbish! Take him away," Bao snapped.

"Have mercy on me, I remember now. During the famine, he gave me a lot of pumpkins."

Alas, that was iron-clad proof of my "crime". It got even worse later when they finally got hold of Kong, whose ex-husband in Hongkong had sent her canned food during the bad years. A reader of detective stories, Bao could weave them himself: An undercover agent, Kong received secret instructions in the cans her husband sent while I supplied her with state secrets. Look, three fifty in the morning, Zhu, wearing an American raincoat and a cap (he hadn't worn a cap that night), smoked five cigarettes in a row. At five o'clock sharp, Gao Xiaoting had appeared with a cart, looked around and whispered, "Let's go. . . ." This detective story had a good beginning and sold well. He was invited to speak at a lot of places. He spun his story out while I had to stand bending over and answer questions too.

"Do you admit your crimes?"

"Yes, I do." And I really did. It had been wrong of me to encourage and promote Bao instead of criticizing him when he came to me with the story about Chef

Yang opening an underground restaurant with a coquettish woman collecting the money when all Yang had done was have a meal at Kong's. If he could get promoted by lying, then what would stop him making up even more lies? The more he gained from telling lies, the greater his lies would be.

"Answer me. Are you guilty of a monstrous crime for which you deserve to die?"

I refused to answer. I didn't want to die. I wanted to live. I wanted to correct my mistakes. I wanted to live for the cause of communism, something for which I would gladly give my life.

Blows rained down on me. They weren't violent but they pierced my heart like daggers. I felt that I had practically placed the dagger in Bao's hand myself.

The neighbourhood committee couldn't just sit doing nothing, so since Bao had dealt with me, they made Zhu, Kong and me confess our mistakes in front of the committee every morning. Zhu and I were finally side by side.

Standing outside the neighbourhood committee with a placard round my neck was worse than standing on a platform being condemned. When I looked down at the large audience I never knew how many of them actually knew me personally. At the neighbourhood committee everyone who went by was known to me. This old lady with a shopping basket had known me since I was a boy, that woman had invited me to her wedding, that boy always called me uncle. I lowered my head and looked at the ground. They would take a detour or quicken their steps, feeling bad at seeing someone who had neither stolen nor robbed standing there like a man sentenced to death. I identified them by their shoes and the way they walked, particularly my mother, whose feet had been bound and later unbound. She'd hovered near me countless times in her life. Now her steps were heavy and hesitant.

A'er paid less attention. As he went by he would cough loudly and then whisper, "Hang on."

Kong couldn't take it. After half an hour, she collapsed and cut her face.

My disgust for Zhu increased tenfold. I stood as far away from him as I could, showing that he and I didn't belong in the same category.

The following morning, A'er came with a big cart loaded with iron and wooden poles and ropes. Twenty burly porters wearing straw hats were following behind. Stopping right behind us, someone demanded, "Who told you people to stand here?"

Frightened again, Zhu blurted out, "The head of the neighbourhood committee."

A'er gestured to one of them. "Go and get him."

Five or six men dragged the man out.

"Did you tell them to stand here?" they asked him.

Sensing trouble, he replied, "May I ask which faction you belong to?"

"The rod faction. You mind that people are not allowed to stand here and block the traffic." The men began to take up their rods.

The committee head tried to calm things down. "We can talk it over, revolutionary comrades."

A'er spoke up: "If you feel you must punish them, then make them sweep the street round that corner."

A man who knew his way around, the head understood his intention at once, and avoiding the beating he might get if he gave them a hard time, he quickly motioned us off. "Go home and get your brooms."

A'er threw me a cheerful glance. "Get going, don't dawdle. And do a thorough job."

I had to laugh. The street they were talking about was a dead end lane of only thirty metres or so, it wouldn't take us long to do it.

But I couldn't escape Zhu, who always tagged along behind me trying to find ways of expressing his gratitude.

"You have a loyal friend," he told me.

I could hardly stop myself blurting out, "Our friendship doesn't come from eating and drinking together."

After a Long Absence

It was a full nine years before I saw Zhu again, during which time I and my family were sent to the countryside. He was probably still living in No. 54.

Nine years is a long time. My own experience, what I saw and heard in those nine years, made me think about the whole issue of food. I passed my fiftieth birthday deep in thought.

On my birthday, my mother killed a chicken and got a bottle of good liquor through a friend. I drank three glasses in low spirits and was suddenly seized with fear. I'd turned fifty before I knew it! After Liberation, when I'd gone to meetings with men in their fifties I'd taken it upon myself to help them up and down steps; to me they were old people. In the country, a man of fifty with filial children did not expect to carry heavy loads any more. "Greying temples but no achievements makes a hero tearful and sad." Though I was no hero, I shed a few tears of regret too. Tearful and tipsy, I let my thoughts run wild. "If I am given a post again, first I want to. . . . Second, I want to. . . ." It was like a dream. Dreams can sometimes come true, but only with a lot of difficulty.

After those disastrous years, I went back to Suzhou, this time not with all my belongings on my back but with my family, my bits and pieces, my furniture and farm tools, which filled a truck. Suzhou felt both familiar and strange. The streets were still the same. But where had all the people come from? Suzhou people preferred window-shopping to going to parks when they had free time. Now, the streets were so crowded you had to pick your way carefully when crossing and if you met a friend you could only shout loudly on the curb while a stream of people continuously brushed past you. The city's population had swollen rather than decreased, although a lot of people and their families had been sent to the countryside. I'd been squeezed out of my home and had to put up at a relative's for the time being. This suited me fine, since I could keep my distance from Zhu, who was in another part of the city.

A man from the organization department came to talk to me. He was about my age. The man who'd wanted to starve me for three days and who'd later become the director of the organization department was no more. May he rest in peace.

"We've been considering sending you back to your old job. How do you feel about that?"

I was overcome by emotion. If that old director had been there I would have broken down right in front of him. You needn't starve me any more, director. I fully realize the significance of food now. And you can relax, Bighead Ding, I won't force cabbage and shredded meat on my customers anymore. I want to work hard and make up for lost time, work for you and for the old director.

"Don't be upset. What's done is done. We've still got a lot to get through."

I nodded. It goes without saying that food supplies are the first thing on the list to be affected whenever there is a disaster. And once the bad times are over, the first place people rush to is the food market; after that they buy their clothing, electric fans and TV sets.

I wasn't wrong in my guess, although I'd overlooked two things. After the ten years of chaos people began to look up old army mates, relatives, former classmates and bosses. Some of them had been held in custody for ten years, others had faded into obscurity ever since the 1957 anti-Rightist movement. People made inquiries: was so-and-so still alive, where were they, etc. Every household had their surprises, "My goodness ... where have you been all these years?" Opponent of eating though I was, I couldn't oppose dinners in such situations. I was human; I had feelings too. If Ding could come and see me now, I would have feasted him for three days running.

One other thing I hadn't foreseen was the rise of tourism. The word "tourism" was never used before and such activities were called "enjoying the mountains and rivers", which had something of a derogatory meaning. Now we gave "tourism" a new meaning — seeing and appreciating the beautiful mountains and rivers of our native land. Anyway, whatever the meaning might be, I had no objection to people going out sightseeing. We particularly welcomed foreign tourists to see our culture and spend their foreign currency. The rockery and pools of the Suzhou gardens might be artificial, but all the earth's culture was made by people. Real mountains and rivers might be wonderful, but they weren't culture; they came from heaven. Besides, with no boasting on my part, the artificial gardens of Suzhou were more characteristic, more concentrated, perfect and unique than real ones.

And what about Suzhou cuisine? Well, manager, in this ancient paradise food was on a par with scenery. Since I wasn't opposed to dinners and tourism and welcomed foreign visitors, my restaurant had to catch up.

We had a hard time in the beginning; my customers just weren't satisfied. Not enough seats, too little variety, bad service, so on and so forth. They criticized and complained. Some had a go at me about it. Once Bao even came to blows with a few young men.

After the fight, he came to me with an embarrassed look on his face. "I . . . I treated you badly in the past, Manager Gao."

I brushed it off. "Forget it, it wasn't entirely your fault. If you've come to apologize, you can stop right now. If you've come about something else, then just say what's on your mind."

Bao hesitated a little. "I've . . . got a bad temper. I don't think I'm much of a waiter; my attitude annoys people. In the past I had some wild ideas about being somebody. I know now that you can only get on in the world if you've got qualifications. So I want to learn some kind of skill."

"You want to quit?"

"No, that wouldn't be very practical. I want to learn to cook. I think I can learn to do it better than others."

"Well." I thought about it. Bao's attitude couldn't change overnight. He might come to blows again. Then again the kitchen was short of hands; we needed more chefs. I gave him my consent.

Bao was very pleased. "You can relax," he told everyone. "That capitalist roader isn't the sort of person to bear a grudge. Although I beat him up before, he hasn't paid me back. Since all you've done is write a few posters about him, you don't have anything to fear."

Don't belittle Bao's declaration. It had the effect of reassuring people. After those chaotic years, people wanted a more peaceful life. If they grumbled a bit, it was because they were impatient for improvement. This was no bad thing. Impatience gave some kind of impetus; it was better than indifference.

We studied the customers' comments book. Apart from our bad service, other things were brought up too, such as the quantity and quality of the food, quick service for those who wanted to go out sightseeing, patience with those who wanted to be left in peace when old friends got together. Some of them placed more importance on famous specialities and others on reasonable prices. Some of them had lost their tempers at having to wait too long, others complained about the cost. My conclusion was that I should neither force cabbage and shredded meat on people nor do away with it entirely, but should improve its flavour.

I introduced foreign ideas into my restaurant by serving fast food — one dish, a soup and a bowl of rice. People could eat quickly and head out sightseeing.

Actually the fast food wasn't much different from ordinary mass-produced food; it just sounded more efficient. I had the ground floor seats changed into booths so it seemed like being on a train.

Young people liked the idea and the lower prices.

When I was young all I knew about was tractors, while they knew about revolving restaurants abroad. How they revolved I had no idea, but my booths had a feeling of motion too. And the fast food wasn't bad: there were also side dishes of fish, spare ribs, shrimps and chicken. One young man even snapped his fingers at me and said, "Hey, bring me a bottle of whiskey." This I didn't agree with; I was afraid whiskey and vodka were more or less the same.

Upstairs we served hot food and the space was repartitioned and furnished with square tables and imitation redwood chairs. Big round table tops could be put on the ordinary tables for large groups. Green plants decorated the corners. Old people nodded in approval, "It's just like it used to be." Actually it wasn't exactly the same, otherwise they would have said, "What's the matter with these people? It's all run down after twenty years."

While I was up to my neck in renovation work, I heard the odd comment drifting by. "In the past this old fellow tore down the partitions. Now he's putting them back again; why couldn't he have been smarter before? My heart sank; I'd become an old fellow. Well, I might be old, but why did they call me "old fellow"? Anyway, my repartitioning was certainly an improvement on the former, only it had taken twenty years to do. That I felt bad about.

Renovating the place and introducing a few foreign

methods was easy enough to do, but traditional cuisine posed a much more difficult problem since our skilful chefs were few. Yang and his peers had all retired. The young chefs were quite ignorant about a lot of traditional dishes and wanted to learn. They'd heard about Yang's skill and were eager to learn from him. They must have heard how I'd treated him too. History is recorded by word of mouth as well as by books.

I decided to look Yang up and ask him to give lectures to the staff, hoping that he wouldn't bear old grudges. We would pay him well and treat him like a professor.

It was raining hard that day, but I decided to go anyway. Yang was quite moved that I'd come in the heavy rain. "You still haven't forgotten me," he said. He'd aged a lot and was hobbling and a bit deaf. When I told him why I'd come and asked his forgiveness about the past he grasped my hand and said, "Save your breath, I've already forgotten. I still think of the restaurant as my home; that's where I learned, that's where I grew up. Whether you'd invited me or not, I'd still have come to visit my old colleagues before I kick the bucket. I've heard you're doing pretty well."

I was moved by his magnanimity. He was still enthusiastic about our work, and his enthusiasm was even greater than mine.

He came accompanied by his grandson. He looked round the place, nodding with approval all the while, saying it was incomparably better than before. Spacious kitchens, refrigerators, ventilators, white stoves and modern cooking utensils — it was better equipped than the kitchen of the foreign affairs office where he'd worked. He studied our menu very carefully.

The whole staff came to his lecture. I asked him to speak openly and concentrate on our shortcomings. He spoke well and had a sense of propriety.

"I'm impressed with your work. Your menu includes almost all of Suzhou's specialities and the cooking is good. Of course you're hampered by the lack of ingredients and the large quantities you have to prepare. But that can't be helped; you've got a lot of people to serve and they don't mind what they spend. I've been told that you've never heard of some of our most famous specialities, which is because one dish can have a lot of different names. For instance, what's rather grandly called the 'supreme dish' is only baked rice soup. . . ."

The audience burst out laughing.

"Yes, baked rice soup, you've got it on your menu, but there are a lot of famous dishes that you can't put on the menu. Take fish lung soup for example. The fish lungs are only the size of broad beans. Where can you buy those in quantity? Actually the lung itself doesn't have much taste; what makes it delicious are the other ingredients and the monosodium glutamate. It became famous only because Yu Youren, a big Kuomintang official, wrote a poem about it after he had it in the Shijia Restaurant. Then both the restaurant and the soup became well-known. Some dishes have become known half from word of mouth and half for their quaintness."

I sat back and heaved a long sigh of relief.

"There are a lot of improvements you can still make. Why kill the fish the day before and keep it in the fridge? Why leave your fresh vegetables in the sun? Everything except your alcohol should be fresh. In the past we took only three minutes from killing a chicken to cooking stir-fried chicken breast."

Bao raised his hand. "Can you tell us the secret of that kind of speed, Master Yang?"

"Actually there isn't one. You just have to have everything ready and work fast. You kill the chicken, plunge it in hot water, pluck the breast only and take the meat. Then dice and stir-fry it. Of course this was a demonstration dish and could make a chef famous."

Yang talked for about two hours and then went to the kitchen to give a demonstration. He was in good spirits and refused to take a break, but he tired himself out and had to rest for a fortnight afterwards.

I'd thought of sending in a report asking permission to have Yang supervise our chefs and be given extra pay. But now I thought I'd better not bother him and just let him enjoy his retired life in peace. However the young people were very enthusiastic and wanted to keep on. I regretted that I hadn't valued their talents and paid more attention to training them. I racked my brains trying to think of a way of making up for it. I asked my staff to recommend good cooks if they knew any. They would be paid well and we would arrange cars for those who needed them.

But alas, this idea was to bring back Zhu Ziye.

A Diner Gives Lessons

I don't know who first brought Zhu's name up, but everybody supported the idea. I was thoroughly surprised that a glutton could be so famous.

I suppose there was every good reason for Zhu to give lectures. He'd been making the rounds of Suzhou restaurants from 1938 to 1958, and before that had frequented Shanghai restaurants too. Though he had nothing to eat in the three lean years, he'd never stopped reading about food. I heard that he wrote a cookbook during that time. Although during the "cultural revolution" he'd confessed to anything put to him, he'd kept his mouth shut about his manuscript, wrapped it in plastic and buried it in a rockery. This action alone put him on a par with scientists, theoreticians and men of letters. Bao put it well: "He could have taught us a thing or two just by telling us what he's eaten all his life." I agreed to do it. I couldn't put my own likes and dislikes above my work any more. At any rate, I hadn't seen him for the last ten years. In ten years a man could become a scholar. But I didn't go and get him myself. Bao went in a taxi. At 68, Zhu was qualified to be picked up in a taxi. Bao said he wanted to take the opportunity to apologize to Zhu and Kong for his past behaviour. I thought it was better for him to make his own apology. People should do their own apologizing. I couldn't take on everything.

I presided over Zhu's first talk. Remembering his fantasies about pumpkins, I wondered what other ideas had occurred to him during the last ten years.

Zhu wasn't a good speaker, particularly in front of an audience. He stuttered and trembled. But when it came to food, he was a different man. He was eloquent, interesting. As soon as he got on stage he asked an interesting question.

"Comrades, who can tell me what is the most difficult thing about cooking?"

The audience's interest was aroused, and they began to make guesses.

"Choosing the ingredients."

"Chopping."

"The actual cooking."

Zhu shook his head. "No, you're all wrong. It's the simplest yet the most difficult thing to do — the adding of salt."

They were all riveted. Nobody thought he'd mention something every little girl could do. When old ladies went to the well to wash rice they would call out to their granddaughters, "Put some salt in the pot for me, would you, dear?" Some of our old chefs nodded in agreement: this simplest yet most difficult thing required great skill.

Zhu elaborated, "Sour in the east, hot in the west, sweet in the south and salty in the north. People all believe that Suzhou dishes are sweet, but actually apart from dessert, Suzhou cuisine is very careful about salt, which enhances all tastes. A fish lung without salt is tasteless. Salt makes the fish lung tasty, ham more savoury, the water shield more slippery and the bamboo shoots crisp. It brings out all these tastes and yet vanishes itself. The right amount of salt is not salty; if there is too much you taste nothing but the saltiness. Then all the skill in the chopping and careful cooking is wasted."

I was astonished that he could be so convincing.

He went on, "The quantity of salt varies with the people and the time. The first few dishes of a banquet should have more salt because the diner's body needs it and his palate is still not ready. The dishes that follow should have less and less salt. The soup that comes at the end of a forty-course meal should have no salt at all and people will appreciate it all the same, because after so much wine and food, the body is already saturated with salt and people need water. And water with a little MSG is delicious."

Zhu interspersed his talk with interesting anecdotes too. "Not putting salt in soup was an accidental discovery by a famous chef. The dinner had been going on from 6 p.m. to midnight and he was so tired he had forgotten to add salt. When he realized and hurried into the dining hall with it, people had already finished the soup and commented that it was the best course of the evening."

He went on non-stop for two whole hours impressing the audience with an extensive knowledge which, like an iceberg, was only showing its tip. He ended to applause and returned to his seat with his chest all puffed up. His ruddy face and silvery hair gave him an air of solemnity. Bao picked his way through the audience and walked up to grasp his hand. "That was excellent, Mr Zhu. I tried to take notes but I missed a lot. Could you repeat what you said if I bring a tape recorder to your home?"

"Well ... yes, but please come after three in the afternoon. I take a nap at noon."

"Certainly. I won't trouble you to repeat your talks in future; I'll just record them right away. Then I'll transcribe them from the recording."

"That's not necessary. I just talk off the cuff."

"It's very valuable information. It would be a pity if it wasn't taken down."

"Well, let me read the manuscript when you've done it."

"Of course, I'd like you to have a look at it."

Since he had after all been to a private university,

Zhu did have something of a professorial air. Bao always liked to collect material, so I asked Zhu to continue his talks over the next few weeks.

Zhu gave three talks. Bao borrowed a four-speaker tape recorder and recorded everything he said. In his second talk, people began to get a little impatient. He went on and on about the importance of adding salt but never told people how to do it. The chefs weren't amateurs like me, they knew the importance of salt. They wanted to gain Zhu's consummate skill of using salt. But unlike Yang, Zhu didn't go to the kitchen to demonstrate. The third time, he began to talk about when and with whom he had a feast on a boat in a lake; how refined the feast of crabs was that he'd had one Double Ninth Festival when they'd used sixty-four solid silver pieces of cutlery to eat them with. And he kept harping on about the dishes today being a far cry from those in the past. I remember how he'd belittled the emperors' palate, but now he was praising the imperial food of the Qing dynasty to the skies. I took it in stride. Food wasn't like works of art, the older the better. A primitive mural found in a cave was precious, but was the ox roasted in a cave in ancient times the best too? The chefs began to yawn and some of them left for home, saying they were fed up with his bragging. In his fourth talk he even started on about singsong girls, flower girls and actors who performed at banquets.

I decided to put a stop to it. Bao protested, saying that history would hold me responsible if I didn't preserve such precious material.

The mention of history left me cold. If Zhu disclosed something valuable in his future talks or if he had already done so and we'd missed it, then I'd take the responsibility. Yet I refused to be cornered now, having learned the trick of not committing myself first. I would wait and see and only speak when things were clear; then I could always be in the right.

"How about this? Zhu needn't give his talks any more because no one wants to listen. You can go on with collecting material since you've already started. I'll provide you with the things you need."

Bao was delighted. "Let's buy a four-speaker recorder."

"No. I'd have to get permission for that. But you can buy some cassettes on our propaganda fee. Don't get all foreign ones only, get some of our Chinese-made ones too."

He was very pleased. "Thank you for your trust in me, Manager Gao. I'll do my best to do a good job."

So the lectures were settled that way. We paid Zhu his fee and the taxi expenses. But the matter was not quite finished. Bao kept on buying cassettes; every two weeks he bought a couple more. When I signed his receipt one day, I inquired, "When will this mission end?"

"My dear manager, it's become a big thing now. I've made contacts for Zhu to give talks at a lot of places, so it's not going to end. Nor do we want it to. We've decided to set up a Culinary Society, so that we can have a proper name when we make contacts. Zhu will be president, I'm vice-president. You're one of the sponsors too. Since you're so busy we thought of asking you to be an honorary councillor."

"What?" My head was spinning. Bao seemed to be

organizing another attack force the way he had in the "cultural revolution".

"I can't," I protested. "I don't know anything about cuisine."

"You don't have to, just give us your support."

"No, we don't have that much money to throw around."

Bao laughed. "Manager, you're such a. . . . You don't need money, we can make money by selling mimeographed notes of his lectures. The street stalls sell sewing books at a hundred percent profit. Cookbooks will sell well too. Besides, we can sell them at Zhu's talks for people to buy with their office propaganda funds."

I had to hand it to Bao; he was a much better businessman than I was. I'd never thought of tapping the propaganda fund, which of course was much easier than taking private money. I had no right to forbid them and could only give them a warning.

"You mustn't have things like singsong girls in your notes."

"We won't. I'll do the actual writing, all purely academic. Nothing about love."

I smiled and signed his bill. "Remember, next time buy domestically-made ones."

"Don't worry, there won't be a next time." He waved the bill. "We're going to buy a four-speaker recorder and a calculator."

I didn't take Bao seriously. They were dreaming. Bao's cooking skills and Zhu's theories about salt didn't warrant research. Bao liked to follow the fashion, he'd turn back after a while.

But I was a bit simple; I underestimated Bao's ability. A good cook he wasn't, but he was an old hand at manoeuvring and gauging situations. Well-known restaurants were gathering places for all sorts of people, particularly well-known ones. You could set up relations by being friendly, giving good service, helping people make orders and reserving seats for them. You could get to know the younger generation if not the older one, and the young could influence their parents. Bao had helped them organize receptions for their sons' and daughters' weddings or get-togethers with old friends. They didn't mind spending money but they just couldn't cook well. Although Bao was no expert, he could get skilful cooks for them. Good cooking, Zhu's boasting and Bao's arrangements would doubtless make the banquets a success. They would explain the aim of their culinary society at these parties and get support. A culinary society which laid sumptuous dinners right before your eyes was more likely to get support than a nutritional society, which was difficult to grasp though it might keep one fit and healthy. The word "society" had its appeal. Anti-academicism had been crushed and now everyone knew a little learning was better than no learning, so you wouldn't be in the wrong by supporting a society. Even if it was a mistake, it was still an academic problem to be thrashed out. And the more you discuss and debate something, the more famous that something becomes.

Zhu's fame grew. He was said to be an expert who had written a book during the "cultural revolution" which had brought manager so-and-so to his knees. This manager had sent a taxi to get him to give lectures and offered him 200 yuan a month to be an adviser, but Zhu had declined.

News of Bao's activities and Zhu's growing reputation reached my ears. "Watch first and make comments only when the time is ripe." Now the time was ripe, yet I had nothing to say. I couldn't say Zhu was just boasting and that people shouldn't pay any attention to him. What was the harm in listening to theories of adding salt? Nor could I claim Zhu had been a glutton all his life and would never change. . . . That would sound more like a compliment, since people who want to achieve something should devote their entire life to their pursuit. There was nothing I could say about Bao either. I couldn't say he was opening an underground restaurant, nor was he asking me to sign his bills any more. I would only be picking up a rock to drop on my own feet. Some people drop that rock as soon as they pick it up, but others drop it dozens of years later.

A Sumptuous Dinner

Not long after that, my old friend A'er came to see me. Even though we were no longer neighbours, we often called on each other. The day I moved into my new place, his whole family came, even his father. "Well, congratulations," he said to my mother. "Now you'll never have to worry about being thrown out by a landlord any more." My mother, who was getting on now, didn't reply and just wiped away tears. A'er often dropped in for a chat, a cigarette or a cup a tea. This was the first time he'd looked me up in the restaurant.

He waved to catch my attention. "I wouldn't have bothered you today, only I wanted to ask you a favour."

"What is it?"

"My eldest son is getting married this Sunday. I tried to book two tables for the reception but was told I'd have to wait three weeks. Can you help me?"

That put me on the spot. "So you do this too. Other people give banquets in restaurants to show off, save themselves trouble at home and collect gifts. Is that what you're up to? How much should I give?"

"Come on, I'm not inviting many people. The bride and bridegroom's family and yours, less than twenty altogether."

"You could have a party at home by putting a couple of tables in your courtyard. Look at this place; it's so noisy you couldn't even hear people's congratulations. Once it gets near closing time, the staff are so eager to knock off they stand next to you holding brooms. How could you possibly enjoy your meal?"

"Listen to you! Running down your own restaurant."

"It's not that; our food's not bad. We get a pile of complimentary letters every month. But I just always feel a party at home is nicer. Besides, we have a regulation that no employee may sit down at a friend's table. Should I just stand beside you and watch you eat?"

"Of course not; this time I want to do something special for you. If you hadn't persuaded me to dig ditches, my life would have been quite different."

"Good. Then have a party at home. I'll get you a good chef, first-rate."

"There's no need," A'er laughed. "We've got a big family and everyone can do something. Times have changed; everyone's got a couple of specialities."

"Splendid, everybody can cook one dish. I'll do the soup."

A'er waved his hand. "Thanks, but don't bother. I know how to do it. You just come over early; I'll be expecting you."

I was really looking forward to the wedding reception. I'd brought trouble to this household once. A'er's father had had to sell ginger and onions because of me. Now, the same courtyard where A'er had promised to give me those pumpkins would hold two tables of food. I felt thoroughly happy.

Just then Bao raced in, looking really pleased. When everyone was happy then the world became a better place.

"Here, manager," Bao cried and thrust a red invitation inscribed with gold characters into my hand. I read, "In celebration of the establishment of the Culinary Society, prominent figures from all walks of life are invited to luncheon on Sunday the twenty-eighth at No. 54, X X Lane." Another dinner party. I quickly said without thinking, "Sorry, I've got an appointment on Sunday. I'm going to a wedding."

Bao scratched his head. "What time?"

"Six o'clock." Another thoughtless answer.

"Excellent. Our luncheon is at noon; there's no conflict."

I looked at the card again. Yes, it said twelve noon. I had to make myself clear. "I can't come. I'm not a member of your society and I'm no sort of prominent figure. It would be inappropriate for me to come."

"My dear manager, your refusal to be our councillor has helped a lot. The councillor's seat is still vacant. Otherwise we would have split up quarrelling long ago."

So my not joining them was an even greater support. How subtle these things were.

"Please come. Everyone's coming; it wouldn't be right if you didn't. Besides, it's not a meeting where you'd have to make a speech. It's just to eat. It would be a shame not to eat such good food."

"I don't care for good food."

"You don't have to eat that much. It would be an eye-opener and a kind of vocational study for you too. To tell you the truth, it's going to be something very, very special. Zhu will give the directions and Kong will be cooking. We've spent four days making preparations. Kong insisted on no more than eight people. We had to do a lot of persuading before she'd agree to use a round table which could seat ten people, including you."

I wavered. Yang had praised Kong's cooking to the skies after eating there. I still didn't know what he'd had that day. I'd regret it all my life if I lost this chance. Besides, I had already given them my support whether I was present or not. If I left a seat vacant once again, what would happen?

"All right, I'll go."

"Fine, then it's decided. I won't come to pick you up. You know No. 54 well."

"I certainly do. I could find it with my eyes closed."

When I'd been in secondary school I went by No. 54 every day and saw the shining rickshaws parked outside the door. Occasionally a Ford would drive up and squeeze the pedestrians against the sides of the lane. The black lacquer door, invariably closed, had a slit and a burglar eye. The slit was a letter box, and the eye enabled those inside to see out but not vice versa. In those days there were a lot of beggars and families had such devices to keep them away. I never saw inside the tall courtyard wall overgrown with creepers, but the scent of osmanthus wafted out in autumn. Now the osmanthus were in bloom again and I had come to No. 54 not as a boy, but as a prominent member of society.

Inside the opened lacquer door stood a beautiful girl in high heels, sleek trousers and a silvery blouse with white ruffles at the throat and a drawstring waist. She walked up to me smiling. I held out my invitation card, but she bowed with a smile and invited me in. "Manager Gao is here, mother," she cried.

So this was Kong's daughter by the politician and professor. Yes, she would have grown up by now; my own daughter was already a mother. I turned to look at her. She was the very image of Kong, who must have been just as beautiful when she was young.

Kong walked along the gravel path lined with flowers. I could hardly recognize her; she seemed to have given her own face to her daughter while turning into a mature lady herself. She had put on weight and looked much younger than when she had stood in front of the neighbourhood committee. She wore her hair piled up high in a pompadour which gave her more height and disguised her plumpness. Her dress was tasteful; time had taught her the art of dressing. A young girl was beautiful no matter what she wore and how she was made up, but the dress of an older woman should bring out her elegance and character. Her simple clothing suited her age and figure and her blue jacket was well tailored and of good quality.

Kong was extremely friendly towards me. People as

meticulous as she was always remembered the small things.

"I was afraid you might not come, Manager Gao. You've got on in years too; are you a grandfather now?"

"Yes, my daughter has a new baby."

"That's nice. Do come in, please, we're waiting for you."

I followed her through a quiet little garden. A stone bridge spanned a square pond on three sides of which were trees, flowers, bamboos and rocks. The bridge led to a big pavilion overlooking the water, which must have been the study of the politician professor. It was spacious and had a long row of French windows opening on to the pool. Looking in, I could see a large round table set in the eastern end, while the "prominent figures" were seated in the west.

Bao came across the bridge to meet me and introduce me to the important people. Among them were two of Zhu's old banquet companions for whom I'd bought food in years gone by. One was a former superior of mine, whose speeches I had listened to when I was a young man. The other three I didn't recognize. One was very quiet; the other two were very talkative and seemed to be businessmen of some kind. Dressed in an old western suit complete with an old tie tucked inside his vest, Zhu didn't look too bad. I didn't know which corner of the trunk he'd dragged the suit out of but it had a strong smell of mothballs. This kind of clothing was familiar to me, but from where? Oh, yes, in my secondary school days my teachers had divided off into two groups. Half dressed in dark blue long gowns and the other half in western suits and leather shoes. My Chinese language teachers were always seen in long gowns and my physics teachers were always in suits. Cuisine was a kind of science. A long gown would be too old-fashioned, an ordinary uniform had no particular impact and there was no particular reason to wear a brand-new western suit. An old suit was just right. He was like an old scientist who had been overlooked for years and had suddenly been discovered by the world. This must have been Kong's handiwork, since Zhu had always been a careless dresser.

Zhu hadn't worn a western suit for ages and seemed a little uncomfortable. He bumped into several chairs and then stuffed a mimeographed manuscript on cooking into my hands. Ill at ease, I sat in front of my former superior. Having worked with him for a period just after Liberation, I was under the impression that he was a sombre and strict person and did not approve of intellectuals. We "petty-bourgeois" elements were always very careful and disciplined in front of him. Meeting him in this setting, I was flustered and at a loss for words, so I slowly leafed through the mimeographed sheets.

"Young Gao."

"Yes."

Then he discovered I was no longer young. "Er, Old Gao, you should read this material carefully and learn from the author."

"Yes, I shall certainly do that."

"Non-professionals cannot direct professionals any more; they really must know what they are doing."

"Definitely. I've made mistakes in the past."

"As long as people recognize their mistakes, there's time to correct them."

I nodded, continuing to finger the manuscript.

Narrated by Zhu and written by Bao, it had nothing new in it and was only copied from a lot of other cookbooks. There were many mistakes, or maybe they were just printing mistakes. I looked up at Zhu, meaning to ask him a few questions, but he avoided my eyes and shooed us all to the other end of the room.

We each politely asked one another to go first and finally persuaded my former boss to take the lead.

The table dazzled us. The white drawnwork tablecloth had been set with an exquisite dinner service: very thin porcelain with a semi-transparent design and a latticework blue rim which looked as if it would leak. There were no flowers on the table but the twelve cold dishes were just as colourful. The shrimp, ham, green pepper, beans and chicken were pretty in themselves. The beef and fish were decorated with all kinds of vegetables, red crabapples and green plums. Salted fish cooked with shrimp roe was usually not good enough for banquets, but since it was a Suzhou speciality and had been unobtainable for many years, it was a rare treat. It was surrounded with white lotus strips partly as decoration and partly to take away the saltiness of the fish.

At the centre of the twelve colourful dishes was a large rose, crocheted perhaps by Kong's daughter, to be used as a mat for hot dishes later on. The entire table was like a large blooming lotus or a water lily or sunflower.

This astonishing sight was greeted by many "ohs" and "ahs".

Another criticism came before we even sat down. "Look at this, Gao, this is real skill. That restaurant of yours is nothing more than a noisy market."

I remained silent and just glanced around. Outside, trees were swaying in the breeze and the reflections of the verandas shimmered in the water as the scent of blossoming osmanthus wafted in. Birds chirped in the garden, just as they had when the politician professor had sat in his studio. . . .

Zhu again urged us to take our seats. He loosened his tie a little and made an impromptu speech.

"Gentlemen, please follow my instructions. There's a lot to knowing how to drink and eat. You mustn't wolf the food, especially at the beginning. Try a little of everything first. The best comes later, so you have to leave some room for it."

Everybody was in high spirits and laughed.

"Although everyone can eat, some people never really enjoy their food. It takes years of experience to learn to do that. I'll explain every dish to you in the hope that you'll give your comments freely. Now let's start; bring the wine glasses."

Bao opened a cupboard and took out a set of wine glasses and two bottles of port. Even without Zhu's explanation I knew one mustn't start with alcohol since it numbed the palate. But I liked alcohol. I'd learned to drink it during the lean years and could drink nothing weaker than 128 proof.

Bao poured the wine into the glasses, making them look instantly like beautiful red rubies.

As vice-president of the society Bao spoke briefly, not so long as to outshine Zhu of course. He raised his chopsticks and urged us, "Let's start, comrades, help yourselves. . . ."

Ignoring Bao, Zhu stopped us, "No, no. You don't tuck into the cold dishes at a sumptuous dinner. They are just to fill the gap between courses so that you can keep on eating and drinking." Then he called out, "Serve the first course."

All eyes turned to the opposite side of the pool. Since ancient times, a gentleman always kept his distance from the kitchen.

I seemed to be watching a film: Kong's beautiful daughter made her way through the trees and bamboos to the bridge. Walking lightly with a tray in one hand, she and her reflection in the water floated toward us like a modern goddess from the Moon Palace. This beautiful scene, directed by that damn Zhu, would make any food in her tray, even if it were only coarse corn buns, seem like one of the Empress Dowager's feasts.

Of course the dish wasn't corn buns, but we were all astonished to see ten scarlet tomatoes when the plate lid was lifted. In Suzhou cuisine, the first course had always been a hot dish like stir-fried diced chicken, fish or shrimps. I'd never seen a meal start with tomatoes. Was this a dish or a fruit?

Zhu served them calmly, putting one on each plate. Then, like a magician, he took the top off of his tomato, which was stuffed with stir-fried shrimps.

In high spirits, we all did the same.

Zhu explained, "Stir-fried shrimps are nothing special; you've all had them many times. Apart from improving the ingredients and way of cooking there haven't been any changes for many, many years. In recent years, people have started stir-frying shrimps with ketchup, but that tastes too western. Shrimps in a tomato are both delicious and attractive, but please don't eat the bowl."

I had to admire Zhu. I'd been wanting to give my customers shrimps for a long time, but it had never occurred to me to stuff them in tomatoes. Autumn tomatoes were expensive, it would be a shame to throw them away. I would have liked to eat the tomato too.

The shrimps did taste better with a hint of sourness from the fresh tomato. Bighead Ding was right in saying that people's palates were more or less the same, unlike Zhu who claimed that some people ate without tasting anything. The difference was that some people could describe it better than others. All some people could say was "Good, superb," while Zhu's talent was in description and exaggeration. He had the ability to exaggerate in a way which could stimulate nerves which had been desensitized by excess.

The goddess floated back and forth across the bridge. I lost count of the number of dishes she brought except that a sweet followed each three. We'd had three desserts already: lotus seed broth, glutinous rice balls cooked with osmanthus and Gorgon fruit with lotus root starch.

I lost interest in Zhu's explanations. The beginning was too superb to be sustained. The later dishes, like hibiscus chicken slices, snowy chicken balls and chrysanthemum fish, could be found on the menu of my restaurant too.

The praises and exclamations were unceasing.

"How did you learn all this, Mr Zhu?" someone asked.

"It's difficult to say; from experience perhaps. You can't learn it from any teacher or book."

"You've had a happy and comfortable life, Mr Zhu. We're much too far beneath you."

"Not at all, we were all in the same boat during the bad years and the 'cultural revolution'."

"That's all in the past now; come on, let's eat."

"All right, when we reach communism we'll eat like this every day."

Hearing that made me feel sick. If we ate like this every day then who would be working, robots? Maybe. But we mustn't start eating right now; the 58th generation of robots was still to be invented.

"Old Gao."

"Yes."

"Why are you so quiet? Did you never discover Zhu's talents?"

"Oh yes, I knew about them a long time ago."

"Then why didn't you ask him to help you improve your restaurant?"

"I . . . did, I asked him to give talks."

"That was only temporary. He didn't have a proper title."

Everyone suddenly fell silent. All eyes turned to me. I was on the alert. Some kind of deal had been planned for this dinner, it seemed.

"What kind of title?" I asked.

"Well, he's a sort of expert."

"What's he expert at?" I waited for an answer. A scientist, writer, actor? He was none of those.

"Eating. . . ." They couldn't go on; that was hardly complimentary.

"Someone who knows. . . ." That was no good. Who didn't know how to eat?

Bao raised his chopsticks. "Foreigners have a term called 'Gourmet'."

"Excellent."

"That's absolutely right."

"A gourmet, a gourmet," they all exclaimed.

"Let's all drink to our gourmet."

Zhu was extremely satisfied, and couldn't resist unbuttoning his old suit and walking round the table to toast me, giving my delicate glass such a powerful clink it almost broke it. This was the high point of his eating life. No one had ever paid him any attention for this lifetime of diligent eating; all he'd had was opposition. His real value was something recognized only by foreigners.

I hated myself for my ignorance, which had enabled Bao to defeat me. All I knew about was introducing fast food and hadn't been on guard for the introduction of gourmets.

People were enthusiastically starting on the tenth course when Kong entered to solicit comments. We thanked her and asked her to have a drink.

"Mrs Zhu, thank you for your superb cooking; thank your daughter too for bringing the food," I said. I wasn't that well disposed towards Kong, but I still had to admit that she was an excellent chef. Actually, she ought to be the president or vice-president of their culinary society. That's the way things were: those who worked weren't up to those who bragged. Those who cooked weren't up to those who ate.

Kong was delighted. "Why, thank you for your compliments, manager." She raised her glass and made a circular gesture to indicate all the guests. "I must offer my apologies to all of you, I'm not satisfied with the cooking I've done. I had to use tinned bamboo shoots since I couldn't get any fresh ones."

"You're being too modest."

"Let's drink to Madame Gourmet."

After everybody had drained their wine, Bao removed the glasses. But this was far from the end of the banquet; he was only changing them.

Zhu produced a set of Yixing pottery wine cups in the shape of peaches with twig and leaf handles. A jar of mild yellow rice wine was brought in. It seemed that the vintage of wine rose with the guests' spirits as the feast advanced. I stole a glance at the two bottles of *wuliangye* in the cabinet. They would probably be opened just before the soup. I wondered who was paying for the meal. Was it Zhu, or somebody's public relations fund?

Kong withdrew to raise the curtain on the second half of the banquet. Hot dishes and desserts came in a stream until a "three-in-one" brought the meal to its climax.

This "three-in-one" was a pigeon, a chicken and a duck stuffed one inside the other and looked like a huge duck sprawling on an oval plate. This was surrounded by quail eggs.

Everyone exclaimed in admiration.

"Old Gao."

"Yes?"

"Now, isn't this the height of perfection?"

"Yes."

"Doesn't this alone make Zhu a qualified adviser for your restaurant with say, a monthly allowance of something in the region of one hundred?"

I realized that this was the crucial topic of the day. I quickly found an excuse.

"That's very flattering, but my restaurant is much

too small to warrant the help of someone so distinguished."

"It's not the size that counts, it's how the manager feels."

Luckily, three-in-one came to my aid at this point. When it was divided up, people were too busy to talk.

I stole a glance at my watch; three hours had passed since the dinner started. There was still my favourite *wuliangye* and a delicious soup to bring it to an end and then there would be fruit. But I dared not stay to the very end; people would chat over their tea and try and put a rope around my neck.

"I'm very sorry, but I have to leave for another appointment. Please allow me to express my thanks to Mr Zhu and to everyone. . . ." I stood up as I spoke, retreating all the time. After I'd gone five steps I hurried across the stone bridge. When I looked back I saw stunned expressions on the faces of everyone in the room.

I had fled in a totally ungracious and impolite manner. Kong would be very hurt if I didn't say goodbye to her.

Kong and her daughter were still busy cooking. When she heard I was leaving, she was disappointed. "Oh, perhaps you don't like my cooking."

"Your cooking is excellent. One of these days I'm going to ask you to talk about it at my restaurant."

She laughed. "It's nothing special, you could do just as well. The only problem is that you don't have as much time to do things meticulously. It takes almost two weeks to prepare things really well. Why don't you stay a while longer? I'm just making the soup. . . ."

I suddenly remembered something. "Mrs Zhu, why

aren't you having a pumpkin bowl for dessert? When your husband came with me to collect those pumpkins he claimed he would invent a pumpkin bowl with a pastoral atmosphere."

"Don't listen to him," she laughed. "All he does is brag."

Chocolates

To the west of No. 54 was A'er's home, where another dinner was waiting for me.

I was already full. The "three-in-one" sat heavily on my stomach and their proposal weighed on my mind. I just wanted to drink a little 128 proof with A'er and his father to warm me up so I could heave a long sigh over the joy, sorrow and hardship of life.

Autumn is the golden season in every city and Suzhou is no exception. This year the temperature was mild, the sky blue and the humidity low. The fragrance of osmanthus drifted out from people's courtyards. The sky above the little lanes was seldom so blue, rarely had so many clusters of white clouds. It was Sunday and the lane was quiet. People were doing their housework, the most important part of which was cooking. Steam floated out of windows which opened on to the street and the sizzling sound of things frying could be heard.

On the way to A'er's I had to go by my old home. It hadn't changed a bit. The black lacquer door, the white walls, the five rooms set back from the street with Zhu's old house behind them. For just a moment,

I seemed to see A'er waiting with his rickshaw at the gate and Zhu coming out in a long gown to sit on the seat, step on the bell and head off to Zhu Hongxing's for noodles. For forty years he had been the incarnation of food, had haunted me like a ghost, had unintentionally decided my career. I hated and opposed him, wanted to keep away from him. Yet instead of getting rid of him, I had been asked to give him a monthly allowance to be my adviser. I would happily give more money to Yang if he could come. But what was Zhu, this man who could only teach people how to squander and waste; what bearing could he have on our work? Just try and squeeze your way in, Mr Gourmet! As long as I'm here you're just daydreaming.

I felt better as soon as I got to A'er's. It was a happy world, with no social rituals, no hypocrisy, no extravagance. The courtyard was full of people cracking melon seeds and eating wedding sweets. My family was already there. My one-year-old grandson was a happy chubby baby who could smile, grimace and wave his plump little hands. Now that each couple could only have one child, each baby had six grownups to look after and admire him. He was the centre of attention. All the guests gave him sweets, talked baby talk to him and passed him round.

Somebody gave him a fruit drop which he pushed out with his tongue.

"Doesn't he like sweets?"

"He does, but he likes good ones."

"Then let's give him a chocolate."

And sure enough the little boy stuffed half the chocolate into his mouth and sucked greedily.

Everyone laughed. "What a clever baby! He likes chocolate."

My head was spinning. When he grew up he would be another gourmet. I had spent my whole life unsuccessfully trying to change Zhu; surely I could change this little creature. I grabbed the chocolate and forced a fruit drop into his mouth.

He started to wail.

Everybody present was stunned, thinking to themselves that this old boy had gone off his rocker.

August-September 1982

Translated by Yu Fanqin

The Doorbell

THERE are eleven main entrance-ways at the east end of the lane. Within some entrance-ways live one or two families, while behind others there are four or five households. The entrance-ways conceal smaller doors and those wishing to enter must first knock at the main entrance. That is why the sound of knocking can be heard day and night at the eastern end of the lane. A knock late at night echoes throughout the lane and, while being rather poetic, is quite devoid of merit in disturbing others' sweet dreams. Happily, progress has been made in the last year or so, for many people have installed electric bells and the frames of the entrance-ways have rows of bell-pushes, all clearly marked with names like Zhang, Wang, Li and Zhao. So if someone forgets their key or a family has visitors the appropriate bell can be rung without disturbing others.

The frame of the eleventh main entrance-way has no bell-push, but within this door without a bell-push is a strange doorbell installed twenty-six years previously by the head of the household Xu Jinghai. This doorbell is a small bronze bell, formerly the trappings of a Buddhist monk, which Xu Jinghai riveted to a sheet of spring steel and nailed to the main door so that when the door opened the spring would jump and the bell sound. The effectiveness of this bell lay not in its role of calling one to the door but as a warning device to alert the inhabitants that someone was coming. And thus all words and actions an outsider should not be party to could swiftly be concealed.

Xu Jinghai put up that bell as a result of the anti-Rightists movement. During that time of struggle which decided the fate of millions Xu Jinghai neither underwent struggle nor did he struggle against others, but he did act to decide his own fate. He learned to play clever, believing that one should not stick one's neck out, nor have any views of one's own or reckless ideas about anything but just study more in one's spare time. Xu Jinghai never had much to stick his neck out over in the first place, so that was not too much of a concern, but judging from what had happened in that movement he felt that was still not nearly enough, especially at home where one's words and actions were rather unguarded. For example, all he did at home was read comics, certainly not study Marxism-Leninism; he was always joking with his wife; and that was even more dangerous! Many Rightists' opinions had been picked up from jokes. Furthermore, in those days Xu Jinghai's wife had still been lively and pretty and enjoyed company, often calling on people while people often would pop in to his house — and it was not until they had got right up close that their host would suddenly discover them. Xu Jinghai found this impossible to guard against and so he adopted an original approach by putting up the warning bell. As soon as the bell sounded everything would be tidied up, a book grabbed or a newspaper taken up for study.

Due to this self-protective attitude of twenty-six years' standing Xu Jinghai had received a hard training, so much so that he had become a shadow; you could say he did not exist but he was all there; you could say he existed and yet there was no sign of any substance. What he said meant as much as not saying anything; if he did not do what he did it would not matter very much. When someone changes from being someone to not being anyone, his aim is to get something from nothing. This might seem a little obscure, but in fact there is no deep mystery. For a number of years we have treated cadres as successful if they have not made mistakes; qualifications and service record come from the accumulation of time, and so every time there is a universal wage increase or a personnel adjustment there has been no reason for Xu Jinghai not to be promoted, let alone the fact that he still studies with dedication. Nowadays Xu Jinghai is the head of a locality, and after one more promotion he will be able to have a room to himself and go first-class when he travels. How many Chinese are able to sit quietly in a first-class compartment on one of those long, crowded, noisy trains going back and forth every day? Some people say Xu Jinghai is a lucky man, surviving by being passive. Xu Jinghai disagrees when he hears this. "What the hell do you know? It's much harder to act passively than to act by doing something. You have to be circumspect, you have to be patient, you have to use your brains all the time, you can't be the slightest bit careless — put one foot wrong and everything will be wasted!" In all fairness, there is some merit in Xu Jinghai's disagreement, for he has been surrounded by dangerous phenomena for over twenty years. Half a lifetime's reputation is not easily attained, and, apart from his own training and experience, he is dependent upon that bell.

The doorbell rings and now the small drama begins. . . .

This is a contemporary play: the time is seven a.m. on a Sunday at the beginning of June in 1984.

When Xu Jinghai heard the bell ring he subconsciously sat up straight in the armchair and took up a newspaper. The point of this action was to show people that he was always busy studying at every hour of the day. However, the time for such motivation was over and it was no longer necessary — it was merely an habitual action, a conditional reflex.

"Dad, there's someone to see you!" Xu Jinghai's youngest daughter, twenty-eight-year-old Xu Dongya, called from the main entrance-hall, her voice at once soft and rather unrestrained.

Xu Jinghai looked at his watch — who could it be this early in the morning? It must be Party Secretary Chen who has retired and lives at the western end of the lane. Secretary Chen goes off to the market every day with a basket on his arm, buys a couple of fish cheap and then comes knocking on the door to boast about it for half the day. He no longer worries about the political meaning of each action but specializes instead in calculating the price of fish, prawns and vegetables. Of course he has not entirely forsworn politics — he always wants to hear a bit of news: whether someone has fallen from power and who has been promoted.

Xu Jinghai lives in an old-style small courtyard house. There is a large courtyard between the entrance hall and the living-room, in the middle of which is a clump of bamboo like a green screen shielding the living-room, so that even if a guest came through the main entrance people in the room would still have time to retreat. Xu Jinghai stood up hurriedly from the armchair, thinking that he would go into the courtyard to stop Secretary Chen's advance and talk outside for a while so that he would not sit down in the armchair and be reluctant to get up again as all the while the stench of fish seeped out from the small shopping basket.

Just as Xu Jinghai stepped over the threshold he saw a riot of colour before him: Xu Dongya was escorting a brightly-dressed man and woman through the green screen. While the man was not young, his face was glowing with health and his hair gleamed. He was wearing a trim brown western-style suit, a cream shirt and a blue tie with white stripes. A diamond pin flashed brightly on the tie. The woman was rather younger and very beautiful, with high-heeled white shoes, flesh-coloured stockings, a dark blue skirt, a light blue blouse and a snow-white crocheted top which resembled white clouds in a blue sky or blue sky within white clouds. She was pulling a large leather case on wheels. The way she pulled the case was very attractive, like a beautiful woman with a dog on a lead.

As soon as Xu Jinghai saw this modern pair his brain began operating on full horse-power: "Who can they be? . . . Ah yes! Some people at work are right in the middle of negotiations with foreign businessmen, but I've never had anything to do with business negotiations, so why should this boss-type turn up here in my house with that woman?" The wary Xu Jinghai became even warier, increasingly vigilant. "I must watch out — there's a sugar-coated bullet in that case — a cassette recorder with six speakers!"

Even though Xu Jinghai was on the alert against

these two, he was still able to put on a pleasant expression and greet them with a smile. Foreign connections were involved and one must be polite; at the same time, because the woman was very beautiful and beauty can usually make one put on a pleasant expression, the smile was not necessarily false. He went forward a couple of steps. "And whom do I have the honour of. . .?"

The gentleman said delightedly, "Old Xu, it's Meng Deyi!" As he said this he flapped the lapels of his suit a couple of times. "Ah! The problem's all with this foreign suit. So you don't recognize me, eh? We used to work together just after Liberation and then I came a cropper during the anti-Rightists movement."

"Oh, it's you!" Xu Jinghai remembered immediately. The reason why he remembered so quickly was because the guest had mentioned the anti-Rightists movement. He had developed the habit of remembering people, events and years through movements — the name of each movement acted like a mnemonic. As soon as the anti-Rightists movement was mentioned the thick account book in his head flipped back several hundred pages and under the entry for anti-Rightists he found Meng Deyi: this man had become a Rightist in 1957 and had been taken back to his ancestral home to be reformed through labour. They had previously been quite close, but after that there had been a complete break and they had had nothing more to do with each other. "Oh! Please, please come in and sit down. Let the woman comrade have the sofa — you can spread out a bit. Go and make some tea, Dongya. Do you smoke? You don't? That's good, it's not good for you. . . ." Xu Jinghai brought out a stream of polite nothings as all the while his brain was still turning over material on Meng Deyi's background. His brain was like a computer with the ability to calculate extremely swiftly and furthermore able to change or add to the stockpile of the past. For example, he no longer regarded Meng Dcyi as a class enemy and even felt some sympathy and gratitude, grateful that he and others like him had acted as a warning vanguard so that he himself had come to understand life's secrets and become successful. Those who fell by the wayside had had a tough time, and even if they had righted themselves and got back onto the road, time had been wasted and their constitutions undermined. Life is like a hundred metre race — when you trip and fall and get up again you come in last. Merely from the point of view of wages you are two to three ranks behind your contemporaries, badly treated; what a shame! "Well! And what wind blew you here today?" Xu Jinghai was still talking in platitudes — he had not yet finished going through the background material.

"A lucky wind. I had to pass this lane on the way to the station and when I saw your doorway I was reminded of old times, so I knocked to ask if you still lived here; I never thought I'd actually be able to see you!" Meng Deyi leaned back in the armchair, his hands crossed over his chest, measuring up the furnishings of the living-room. He was like someone who had travelled far across the oceans and returned to his original port, feeling that it was particularly peaceful and comfortable and that to live happily here in this small place for many years was good fortune. "Not bad, old Xu. I heard you've done all right for yourself over the years — your children all grown, an important job; your 'historical task' is almost completed!"

"Not at all — much less than other people! What important job? I'm just a middle-level cadre, that's all. As for the kids — I'll never be finished with their problems. Just look, all these years and I'm still living in this old place." Behind every word Xu Jinghai spoke there was another layer of meaning: "Of course! Compared to you I'm in heaven! My job's not so unimportant either — with one more promotion I'll be in the ranks of senior cadres. My children are all doing well. And as for the house — well, just wait awhile. As soon as this wind's blown over the problem will be solved. But I don't want to move — it's more relaxed living here in this small courtyard." Xu Jinghai did not say this out loud and did all he could to keep his tone subdued. He could not say his situation was too good but had to avoid the envy and jealousy of those who had suffered; nor could he say his position was too important because it would be difficult to refuse someone if they asked a favour. There are not many coincidences in this world, and Meng Deyi's knocking at the door so early in the morning had to be because he wanted something. Even if he were not giving a sugar-coated bullet he could still probably raise a difficult problem which it would be best to try and avoid. Xu Jinghai's computer went into operation again: in order to deal with a possible problem he must continue looking through the background material. Under the heading anti-Rightists he discovered that all those labelled Rightists had some kind of fault — some thought too highly of themselves, some liked to be in the limelight, some couldn't keep their mouths shut and some were pigheaded. Meng

Deyi's faults were even greater. When he was young he had been unable to know his place, he had had an exaggerated opinion of himself and was always doing things people did not expect. There was the year he was sent off to a factory on business and he wanted to meet the Party secretary there right away. The secretary had not wanted to meet him and the security man kept him outside. So finally he colluded with the driver of a leading cadre, was driven into the factory sitting in the official car and went straight up to the Party committee's office. The Party secretary was uncertain whether or not he was an important official and so chatted politely with him for an hour. In the fifties he pretended to be an important official and in the eighties a Hongkong businessman — who knew what game he was playing! Xu Jinghai looked at Meng Deyi and uttered some more platitudes: "How long have you been here? Five days eh? Quite some time!" Five days and doing what? With his hair all smooth and slickly combed, wearing a trim western suit and bringing a beautiful woman along with him! It looks as though there is something close about their relationship — the matter bears some looking into. Xu Jinghai himself did not understand why he was interested in such matters but he still asked, ". . . Er, I forgot to ask who this lady comrade might be. . . ?"

"And I forgot to introduce you. This is my wife, Dong Bei." Meng Deyi spoke with confidence but discovered right away the glint in Xu Jinghai's eyes and the astonishment on his face, and his smile became rather forced. Meng Deyi had seen this phenomenon many times and he knew that if he had brought along an old wife much the worse for wear everyone would consider it normal. It was not all right to have Dong Bei: those astonished glances were always prying for some sort of immorality. While Meng Deyi could not care less about this, Dong Bei could not take it and so he had to say something in explanation. "Perhaps you remember that my first wife flew the roost after I'd been made a Rightist. I was single for over twenty years and only remarried three years ago. Don't be fooled by her looks — she'll be fifty very soon!"

Dong Bei smiled winsomely and nodded her head. Apparently she liked to get herself up to look younger than she was and yet also liked people saying she was older.

Xu Jinghai was a little disappointed. (Why?) He had often seen on TV or in films how all Rightists had beautiful women with them, but originally he had believed it a fabrication and had not thought it might actually be true! Even though this guy Meng Deyi had some tough times it seemed as if he had come off lightly — he looked as though he had been in a freezer for over twenty years and had come out looking as fresh as before, with a lovely wife and himself dressed in western clothes and leather shoes. It's quite true that someone wearing western clothes looks somehow younger and more vigorous. Xu Jinghai had once thought of having a western suit made but on reflection did not quite have the courage, for wearing a western suit brought one a bit too much into the limelight. Besides, his once lively and attractive wife was now old and fat with no interest in getting herself up nicely, so if they went out together they would not match. A couple like Meng Deyi and his wife were unique among their contemporaries. Unfortunately Meng Deyi was not of very high rank and a beautiful wife like that would need money to spend — she certainly would not worry over how much a catty of fish or prawns would cost; when she went out she would want to use a car, she would not want to squeeze onto a public bus. Xu Jinghai could not help glancing at Dong Bei. "You must be tired from travelling. Trains are very crowded these days." It was almost as if he wanted to see how this beautiful woman with the large leather bag would get squeezed on all sides in the door of the train carriage.

Dong Bei smiled but did not reply.

Meng Deyi, however, replied casually, "It's all right. We go first-class." "Ah. . . ," said Xu Jinghai, forgetting to close his open mouth as he said to himself, "Even I can't go first-class; how do you manage it? There was an announcement recently about claiming expenses for going first-class — you have to follow the regulations and there are stricter controls."

"Ah!" Xu Jinghai took advantage of his open mouth to say it again. "Where have you been staying?" This was by no means a superfluous question but indeed the crux of the matter.

"At the Tianran Guesthouse on the seventh floor, room 7021."

Xu Jinghai closed his mouth and opened his eyes wide. What! The seventh floor of the Tianran Guesthouse was famous as a seventh heaven, and 7021 was a large suite in which he had once been received by a minister. Even if you have money you cannot stay in a suite like that, and if you do stay there you cannot afford to pay for it. Xu Jinghai was extremely familiar with the treatment cadres receive: for most of his life he had been quietly and circumspectly climbing those stairs. He knew a cadre's rank was not signified by clothes or food but by accommodation and means of travel. Clothes and food do not clarify matters — a worker of the second lowest rank can wear western clothes, a layabout can hold a banquet. But accommodation and means of travel are something else entirely: there are rules saying what kind of cadre lives in which house, rides in which car, enters which hospital and even where his ashes are put, because all this comes under the category of accommodation. All you need do is clarify a cadre's accommodation and means of travel and you have a fair notion of his job and rank.

Xu Jinghai was confused (why?) and immediately began operating his computer: impossible! There had to be a mistake! When Meng Deyi was made a Rightist he was the same rank as himself, the eighteenth administrative grade; this he remembered distinctly and certainly could not be mistaken in. He might be able to forget someone's age but he certainly could not forget their rank. He had also not forgotten that when Meng Deyi became a Rightist he had been demoted three ranks, going from the eighteenth to the twenty-first grade, and it was just that point which had scared him into putting up the doorbell. Meng had been rehabilitated now but he would still only be able to return to the eighteenth grade; there were fixed regulations on that. There had been two pay adjustments in recent years, but at best Meng Deyi would only get to be fifteenth grade and would not be able to stay in a suite or go first-class. Yet despite this one could not be sure that Meng Deyi was simply boasting — everything was topsy-turvy these days, high-class limousines could be hired and peasants could stay in fancy hotels, just as long as they could bear to part with the money. Meng Deyi had once enjoyed pretending to be a leading cadre and it was natural that he would pretend to be wealthy before a beautiful woman. Xu Jinghai looked at Dong Bei again and noted how her hands rested on her knees. A smile was on her lips and her head at an angle, like the statue of a goddess. But a goddess is no god of wealth — who would be able to consider money in front of her? How could anyone bear to stuff her into a hard-seat train carriage or a shared hostel bed? Still, there was something that still needed to be clarified: was this trip paid for privately or was it at public expense? If he was paying for himself then he was just pretending to be rich to ingratiate himself with a goddess. If it was at public expense then it was unusual and revealed that the vehicle in front that represented Meng Deyi and which had once fallen by the wayside had somehow changed motors and suddenly overtaken and gone beyond his own cart, which had never fallen at all.

"Did you come here on business or are you travelling for pleasure?" Xu Jinghai's question was very apposite — business meant at public expense while travelling for pleasure meant paying one's own way. Of course, there were trips for pleasure taken at public expense but they came under the category of business too.

Meng Deyi laughed bitterly. "What time do I have for pleasure trips? We came here to participate in a meeting inviting tenders in construction engineering. What a struggle that was! It was only last night that we managed to get the contract into our hands." Meng Deyi could not suppress a yawn — he suddenly felt exhausted, not only because of the tension of the preceding days but also because Xu Jinghai was constantly bringing up a spate of boring topics. To accidentally meet an old colleague again and yet not hear a single warm word....

Xu Dongya at last brought in the tea (after a long wait), saying as she walked in, "Oh dear, I really had to boil water for company. Every thermos was empty when we got up this morning so I put the small kettle on to make the tea — I've brewed it strong with boiling water the way my father likes it — aunty, there are less tea-leaves in this cup so you should have it because women don't like strong tea — it turns your skin as brown as an earthenware teapot if you drink too much." There was no punctuation in Xu Dongya's speech — it all came out in one lively stream.

Meng Deyi became livelier too and stood up to exchange cups with Dong Bei. "Let her have the strong cup. These days the most fashionable skin colour in the world is brown. European women spend a fortune to go to the beach to turn brown all over."

Xu Dongya burst into giggles, "What a guy you are for jokes!"

"What's all this about 'a guy'? You must say 'Uncle Meng' and 'Aunty Dong'. At your age and you still don't have any respect for your elders!" Xu Jinghai had some respect for Meng Deyi: he had slotted the western suit, first-class carriage, hotel suite, contract etc. into his computer and the terminal had immediately come up with the information that Meng Deyi was in foreign trade. A rank had recently arisen among cadres of people with know-how and a knowledge of foreign languages who could do business with foreigners. In order to get them to earn more foreign currency, in certain respects their treatment did not adhere strictly to their grade. Although Meng Deyi was not a high cadre, the vehicle which had once toppled was now fitted with an imported motor so that it was sure to travel very fast.

Xu Dongya felt a little aggrieved at getting a lecture despite her good intentions towards the guests. "Next time guests come and you tell me to make tea I'll ignore you!" She turned and went to sit on the sofa, impatiently uttering a greeting to "Aunty Dong".

Dong Bei smiled and took Xu Dongya's hand. Although she said nothing her attitude was very warm.

Meng Deyi made a gesture with his hand. "Don't bother calling us that — standing on ceremony's too cold. How old are you, young lady?"

"Twenty-eight."

"Married yet?"

"Not yet."

"That's right — these days it's not so easy for older young ladies to find a husband. Lower your sights a bit, young lady!"

Xu Dongya livened up. "Huh! Who'd have thought that someone like you, uncle, with your sense of humour, wouldn't understand social problems. You must know it's not hard to find a husband but it's not so easy to find somewhere to live."

Dong Bei smiled, swept a glance at Meng Deyi and leaned closer to Xu Dongya to show that she concurred with the young woman's opinion. The beautiful woman seemed to like substituting light smiles and small movements for words.

Meng Deyi raised both hands. "Good! You've made a good point. You've shown the other side of the problem, but it isn't a problem the daughter of Xu Jinghai should be raising. Old Xu, it seems as if your 'historical task' is not yet over after all. If I had such a lovely young daughter I'd be going all out for her!"

Xu Jinghai sighed. "There's no way. I can't compete with you. You must be in foreign trade these days or the manager of some joint venture?"

Meng Deyi smiled. "Well, I'm certainly a manager, but not of any joint enterprise. Our company's rather different: at the most it could be considered a large collective. I'll tell you — when I was rehabilitated they told me to go and be a teacher, but that didn't suit me at all so I didn't comply. That meant automatic abandonment. Fine! Abandon me if you want; I've already been abandoned all those years, and this time I couldn't give up on my own speciality any longer. I studied civil engineering at university in order to devote myself to building homes for the people. So I went and persuaded the commune secretary to let me first organize a contractors' team out of a few people who used to go stealthily into the city to be construction workers. We borrowed an account number and went into business. In less than a year we'd earned over 200,000, and after turning over a share to the commune some people got as much as two to three thousand each!"

Xu Dongya was fascinated by this account, feeling that here was a man prepared to get on with things. She was just thinking of saying something when she was prevented by pressure from Dong Bei's hand telling her not to talk but to let Meng Deyi continue. Dong Bei was very familiar with the story of her husband's pioneering undertaking and was both sympathetic and admiring. She knew that the part of the story which followed was a tale of harsh experience which was enough to make one weep or even write a novel!

Unfortunately Meng Deyi had never thought of writing a novel and this time, moreover, he did not mention those parts most capable of moving people.

"We're no longer just a contractors' team but are called the Hongda Construction Company, enlisting people from three counties, our staff numbering four to five thousand. Our teams can be found as far north as Xinjiang and as far south as Shenzhen, and we've got over a dozen vehicles of all sizes!"

"Uncle Meng, let me work with you!" cried Xu Dongya.

"Fine! Welcome! But if you joined us . . . what could you do?"

"At the factory I work with technical data and I know some English."

"That's excellent! We are planning to establish a technical data centre but unfortunately don't have the people. Really, first take our company test and then apply to leave your job. It's possible to change jobs these days, so move on over to us and go up a grade, with extra bonuses." It was as if Meng Deyi was cozening a child as he said into Xu Dongya's ear, "Let me tell you, the bonuses won't be far off your wages! How about that?"

Xu Dongya giggled. "I don't want a bonus, just an apartment!"

"An apartment. . . ." Meng Deyi scratched his head. "Fine. You can stay with us temporarily and next year I'll guarantee you an apartment — not too big, one big room, one small, a good size hallway, a kitchen and a washroom."

"Is there room in your house?" It seemed as if Xu Dongya really wanted to go.

"No problem. My home's bigger than this and I'm often not at home so it's lonely for your Aunty Dong to stay there by herself. In fact, if you wanted to get married this year you could set up home in our place first and get Aunty Dong to help you — don't think all she can do is smile; she's great at choosing clothes and furnishings for a home!" Dong Bei smiled and nodded, holding Xu Dongya lightly as if she had already got a companion or found a daughter.

Xu Dongya burst into peals of laughter and half leaned back into Dong Bei's embrace.

"Dongya! Behave yourself!" Xu Jinghai was angry, but it was really Meng Deyi with whom he had a bone to pick: You so-and-so, you're not in foreign trade at all, nor do you have what it takes to earn foreigners' money. You've just reverted to your old ways; it's hard to change your nature. You don't obey when you're allocated a job, you borrow an account number, you trickster, and now you want to drag my daughter into it too!

". . . You! When will you learn to behave yourself better?" Xu Jinghai suppressed his anger, transforming it into resentment. There was nothing to be done. These days the more tricks you played the more complacent you became, as well as earning yourself a good reputation as a reformist! Everything was topsy-turvy. The long line of cadres no longer advanced as a queue; some were now beginning to appear who could turn somersaults, one somersaulting 108,000 *li*, changing in one blink of an eye from the tail of the line to the top. Not increasing his wages made no difference, for people like him could call their own shots and, what is more, you knew how much his limitless bonus was, for it had to be enough for that beautiful woman to spend. Otherwise why would she simply smile and say nothing, not like his own wife always grumbling away crossly, one minute complaining that there is not enough money, the next saying the house is too crowded?

Dong Bei smiled once again, raised her white arm and glanced at her small gold wrist-watch.

Meng Deyi stood up immediately. "Old Xu, we have to get going. Our train leaves at 8:40."

"What!" Xu Jinghai was rather disappointed. Originally he had thought Meng Deyi must want something, coming to call so early, but he had not wanted anything after all and really had just popped in on passing by. "Oh dear, can't you stay a bit longer? Let Dongya ride over to get the tickets and you can have something to eat before you go. We haven't seen each other for twenty years, and who knows when we'll get another chance." Xu Jinghai genuinely did want his guests to stay on, especially since there was nothing about which to remain on the alert and it would be very interesting to talk about old times.

Meng Deyi felt regretful too, having sat for an hour and only now hearing some words with the semblance of humanity in them. "Can't do it — someone's waiting for us at the station and there's a whole pile of family matters too. Frankly, I'd really like to stay here quietly in your little courtyard. No telephone ringing, no urgent telegrams and no one sitting outside waiting to discuss things. Sometime you must come to our place and see all the hustle and bustle for yourself." Meng Deyi took out a card from the pocket of his western-style suit.

"This is my address. Give me a call before you come and I'll send a car to the station to meet you. Ring this number during the day and the second number in the evenings — the second one is my home number." So saying he turned to Xu Dongya to bid her goodbye: "Young lady, if you really want to come you can count on your Uncle Meng."

As he held the card in his hand Xu Jinghai felt as if he had suffered a crushing defeat (not necessarily). Not only did this so-and-so have a house, a car and a beautiful wife but also a home phone! Even if he were to be promoted one grade it was still not certain that he would get a phone. . . .

After the guest had gone Xu Jinghai paced back and forth in the small courtyard, feeling for the first time that it was too small and the air unfresh; his whole body felt uncomfortable.

The doorbell rang again — the little play was not yet over.

When Xu Jinghai heard the doorbell ring he thought that Meng Deyi had come back — perhaps that beautiful woman had left her handkerchief on the sofa. He rushed to the door to see but no, he was wrong, for Xu Dongya was there with her hand against the main door and outside the door was standing Secretary Chen who lived at the western end of the lane.

Secretary Chen, his face covered with sweat, carrying a shopping basket, had not yet entered before producing a large Mandarin fish. "Old Xu, guess how much this fish cost!"

Xu Jinghai was not in a good mood. "Okay, okay, go home quickly and cook it. It'll go off if you leave it too long." Both hands grasping the doorjamb, he blocked Secretary Chen on the outside.

"Hey, hey, what's all this? Had another squabble with your wife? This fish. . . ."

"You've saved thirty cents on it, right? Some people think nothing of spending three thousand!" flared Xu Jinghai, shutting the door with a bang. This was too much for the doorbell which could not take such treatment, falling to the ground with a clangour. The bell had been up too many years, its screws were rusty and the door panels rotting a little, so it could not handle a shock of this kind.

Xu Dongya picked up the bell. "What shall we do with it?"

Xu Jinghai waved his hand. "Forget it — take it to the scrap heap. I'm not going to watch my every movement from now on."

Xu Dongya gave a joyous skip. "Right! The stupid old thing should have fallen off long ago. Let's install an electric bell, one that will play a tune." As she said this she made as if to throw the bell into a corner.

"Hold on!" After all, Xu Jinghai had had over twenty years of training and could do nothing rash. "It . . . it'd be better to put it back up again."

Xu Dongya gave a flounce. "I'm not going to do it!"

Xu Jinghai shouted, "Put it back up! Those who don't follow a normal route will always come a cropper one day!"

The Xu family's doorbell is still safe and well, the monk's trappings still nods its head a little. . . .

Suzhou, August 12th, 1984

Translated by Alison Bailey

A World of Dreams

I have been to many places but the world of my dreams will always be the small lanes of Suzhou. I have walked through these lanes a myriad times and passed much time in them; it is as if my youth had flowed away from these lanes carving a deep gully in my mind, leaving me with a profoundly enduring impression.

Thirty-eight years ago, clad in a long blue cotton gown and riding in a wooden sailboat, I sped up to a small lane outside Suzhou. The lane was paved with long flagstones underneath which flowing water gurgled. It was known as a thoroughfare but it was impossible for two rickshaws to pass each other; on each side there were low one-storied houses, and bamboo poles used for drying washing stretched from the eaves on one side to eaves on the other. Above the eaves were square brick blocks with holes in them which looked just like archers' slits in an ancient wall.

After turning a corner the lane changed; on each side there were now higher buildings with black tiles, crimson railings and white walls. Bordering the lane was a long wooden gallery, the eaves of which were inlaid with painted boards, each carved differently, some with squirrels and grapes and some with the legendary eight immortals who crossed the ocean. Perhaps pretty colour fades easily, for both the crimson railings and the painted carving had already turned black or yellowed with age. Bamboo clothes-poles were slotted within the carved boards and bamboo blinds hung down, concealing windows. It seemed to me that I had seen something similar to this in a scroll-painting or a novel.

There were shops in these lanes as well with living quarters above and the shop itself below. The majority were tobacconists, grocery stores and the kind of teahouse that also sold boiled water. The teahouses were the busiest and noisiest of all, for there were always lots of men there, their left hands on the table-tops, their right feet sticking up on the long benches, holding up those shiny dark brown earthenware teacups and pouring that dark brown water down their gullets with relish. People in Suzhou call this phenomenon "flesh covering water", whereas the evening bath is known as "water covering flesh". The tea-drinkers all naturally wished to engage in elevated discussions, but in the overall buzz of sound it was impossible to distinguish what was being discussed. Only the sound of vendors' cries stood out clearly. These were the girls with baskets peddling melon seeds, sweets and cigarettes. And then there were the blind men in dark glasses playing the *erhu*, huskily singing something. I say "singing", but it came closer to weeping than anything. This small lane unrolled before me like a scroll-painting of life in a market-place.

At the end of this painting I climbed up into a small building. In fact it had two parts, divided into a building at the front and one behind, with wings on either side connecting them to form a square. The courtyard was as small as a deep well, with only two jars for collecting rain-water. If you leaned out and looked down from the front building you could see people going back and forth, a bustling market-place; leaning out of the window in the back building you could see a big river flowing below. On the river sculls creaked, the sky was bright, waves rippled and the wind and sun seemed somehow unhurried. On either bank of the river were people's homes, each house having a long window by the river and a stone jetty. The jetties were built in a marvellous way, simple yet ingenious, using rows of many long stone slabs. One end of each slab stood out in space while the other end was embedded into the long stone wall along the river's edge. The slabs advanced in ranks towards the riverbed, like stone ladders hanging from the back door of each household. Women washing vegetables or rice would ascend or descend the heights of the ladder, appearing and disappearing in the shimmering light and the cloud shadows. Small single-oared boats would move slowly out into the current, letting it take them where it would, their holds filled with fish, shrimps, vegetables or melons. And if someone indicated from one of the windows bordering the river that they wished to buy something, the little boat would shoot over like an arrow. When the transaction was completed a basket with money in it would be lowered from the window, filled with the goods bought and hauled back up again. Then the window would be shut with a creak and the little boat slowly followed the waves once more.

Opposite the building at the back there was a fork in the river spanned by a very high arched bridge, the balustrade of which was a stone wall which curved like a melon seed. When people crossed the bridge only their heads would appear above it. The bridge itself was exceptionally broad, having within its arch on one side an old Buddhist temple, and if I stood on a pier and looked within I could still make out the word "Namah . . . " on the yellow wall. On a moonlit night you could see the swift flowing current within the arch, a sheet of shimmering silver, and the moon's reflection fragmenting, while the temple bells spilled out after the waves of light. A poetic quality was given to these back lanes too by the stone jetties suspended between moonlight and shimmering waves, on which the noise of women pounding washing formed a chorus — "On a moonlit night in Chang'an/There is the sound of a myriad homes pounding clothes." I turned and went back up into the building at the front. I saw the well-lit lane with the rickshaws rattling past, *wonton*-sellers banging bamboo clappers and sellers of spiced tea-flavoured eggs carrying small stoves in large baskets. At night the teahouses became places for storytellers and then the strumming of *pipas* was accompanied by the soft lilting of the Suzhou dialect. Suzhou-style storytelling and ballad-singing were high-pitched and beautiful, and the vending cry of those selling spiced tea-flavoured eggs was filled with sadness. I had not realized that a small winding lane could change so infinitely, be so different within and without, with its rows of houses dividing land and water, silence and movement. On one side was the world with all its joys and sorrows and its hubbub; on the other side were wave reflections and moonlight, and also that low, reverberating sound of an evening Buddhist bell, making it seem as if the world in its entirety could be forgotten.

I once lived in another kind of lane with high surrounding walls on either side, so high that one had to crane up to see the top; no pink apricot could reach out over these walls, for only the spring vines were able to climb up and hang in tassels over the top. The heavy main gates were always tightly shut so that not one morsel of information could squeeze out. Two mounting blocks like strange beasts lay on either side of the gates, glowering at the screen wall opposite, sombre and fierce. The screen wall had a carved stone border and a plain centre. There were few passers-by in lanes such as these, but occasionally a flower-seller would utter a long drawn-out cry: "Who will buy my white orchids?" For the rest, there were only the sparrows cheeping and chattering on the gate-house and magpies hopping on and off the eaved walls. It was as if it was still possible to see princelings or the scions of high officials ride into the lane mounted on fine steeds. The black lacquer gate with brass door-knockers would creak open while four servants waiting within the gatehouse would immediately leap up to help the princeling step onto the block and slide off the horse, which would then be led off and tied by the side of the screen wall. Or you could almost hear the sound of horns and incessant firecrackers and see lanterns and decorations hanging at the gate and a bridal sedan-chair being carried into the lane. And after a few years a memorial to a widow's fidelity or chastity would be raised where that bridal chair had passed. In the yellowing pages of local records it would perhaps be possible to find the name of that upright, moral woman, but the memorial would already have fallen, leaving only two large square stone pillars still standing there.

I brushed past those stone pillars as I entered the lane and stopped before the door of a building. A bamboo plaque was nailed to this door, which was never closed, and an old tailor-cum-watchman did his business in the entrance-hall, watching the entrance for a reduced rent. There was sometimes not a tailor but an old woman with poor eyesight who wore glasses and bent over an embroidery frame, embroidering dragons, phoenixes and bright butterflies. She was one of those ageing seamstresses who spent their whole lives making bridal clothes for others, and even though her eyesight was going, when wearing glasses she could still split coloured silken threads into eight strands. Within entrance-halls of this kind there were often six-leaved doors, some cream-coloured, some with gold-leaf on a dark-blue ground, but here the gold-leaf had turned black in many uneven blotches. Only the first leaf of the door was open so that it was impossible to see at one glance what went on within. I slid inside but still did not see very much on entering, coming instead into a dark, dim world, a long, narrow, seemingly endless corridor. There were many arched entrances and small doorways on either side of this corridor, but each was shut tight, with only a faint light filtering out from windows dispersed far between. Peering on tiptoe through the windows I could see a row of halls down the left side, all dark and gloomy, while on the right side there was a series of courtyards with rockeries, tall bamboos and small buildings with crimson balustrades — a green and shady place. This had once been the home of a wealthy family in which each wife, concubine, son and daughter had their own quarters with a garden attached.

I once spent half a year living in a certain garden which was almost one-third of an acre in size. It could be described as either a courtyard or a flower garden, for this tiny space had all the characteristics of a park, with an artificial hill made from a pile of rocks brought there from a lake. On top of the hill there was a cobble-stone path which twisted and turned, dipping and rising abruptly, one moment passing through a cavern, the next crossing a small bridge over a gully; the gully was just a chink and the bridge was small enough to resemble a model. If you were to follow the curves of the path the distance would be surprising, but if you were to go straight up to the top of the hill it would only be a matter of four to five paces. The hill-top was masked by towering old trees through which the sunlight shone down in rays of gold while everywhere dappled spots of light and shade flickered. There was a lotus pond at the foot of the hill with a crooked stone bridge across it. The crooked bridge was connected to the gallery, which in turn was connected to the water-side pavilions and then curved back to join up with the small building which served as my living quarters. On a rainy day you could stroll along the gallery and watch the raindrops on each layer of branches and leaves shatter into fragments and see a fine shrouding rain submerge all the buildings and pavilions in mist. If you sat in a pavilion for a brief rest you could see the pond slowly flooding until the little crooked bridge was buried beneath the water.

The garden was wild and unkempt; there was white guano on the ground and the caves were the haunts of foxes. Apart from the birdsong, the most animated thing there was the lotus pond: there the plants grew luxuriantly, crowding the water-lilies up against the low embankment, and in early summer charming little tadpoles floated in the clear water within the rock crevices. The pointed tip of the lotus leaf seemed in-comparably sharp, capable of poking up between other thickly growing aquatic plants and boring out onto the water's surface in the space of one night. Yet there were some which did not make it, for carp are very fond of soft, young lotus leaves. At night, the pond was even more active, the croaking of frogs was like drumbeats, now loud, now silent, and in the time of silence you could hear a fish spouting. With a great whooshing sound a large fish leapt out of the water, startling awake the sleeping birds in the trees so that they twittered restlessly. Peace came again only when the croaking of the frogs rose once more. It was very lonely living in that high-walled, deeply receding courtyard with only books for company. I often sat on the artificial hill and read, becoming so completely immersed that several ants would climb up onto me. One mustn't squash that breed of ant for they had a strange smell like powerful turpentine, making me think they had grown up feeding on the resin of the pine tree.

Comparatively speaking I prefer another sort of lane, one filled with life's piquancy and combining all the characteristics of the various lanes together. A lane with high-walled, receding courtyards and low one-storey dwellings; with tobacconists, flatbread-makers and shops selling boiled water. Behind certain facades lived several dozen families and the entrance-halls were comparatively small. At the end of the lane there would be a public well while within the lane the stone pillars once supporting memorial plaques would still be standing. A lane of this kind would have a canal running alongside it but it would be very different from those outside the city, with houses pressing desperately close together on either bank, squeezing the canal so that it became a narrow water channel. A scene of this kind was already familiar to the Tang dynasty poet who wrote, "There is little spare space in old palaces / And many small bridges span the water channels."

When one entered a lane such as this on an early summer morning a mist would be lifting and there would be a group of women drawing water from the well at the end of the lane, languidly pulling up the rope attached to the bucket as if still drowsy from the previous night and still clad in voluminous striped pyjamas. In fact the entire lane had awakened long before this. The retired old men had already gone off to the tea-gardens in the parks or to some teahouse to practise shadow-boxing, drink tea and chat. Those too old to leave home anymore would potter in their courtyard, tending their miniature landscape gardens or sitting blankly in a rattan chair pouring cup after cup of strong tea down their throats. The housewives would already have whisked through their chores and left for the small, noisy food market with a basket on their arm. They would bustle into the small lane, discussing whether or not there were any certain kinds of food available and if they were good or bad, cheap or expensive. It was only after the bell of the rubbish cart sounded that people returned from the market one by one, the morning struggle to buy food now over.

Not long after the food-buying brigade dispersed, activity in the lane would reach another peak. All those off to work seemed to come crowding out almost at the same time, some leaving the lane and heading eastwards, others entering it and going towards the west. Those with satchels were bouncing and full of energy, those carrying children told the kids to say goodbye to their grandmothers. The flashing gleam of bicycles and the ringing of bicycle bells were only common sights. The lane became a bicycling arena or exhibition in which insufficiently skilled females had no choice but to push their bikes through the lane before mounting. And yet this peak was like that of a wave, settling back quietly after half an hour.

When those leaving for work or school had gone, the tea-drinkers and shadow-boxers began to return. As these people entered the lane they were unhurried, their bearing calm and their eyes half-closed as if there were nothing left to startle them here. For them the greatest joy was marriage; the greatest sorrow, death; the greatest factor for alarm was fire and the most frightening thing was the sound of guns. They had been through it all and nothing confounded them. If you were interested in the things that they were not, the experience of each one of them was worth hoarding. Some had been famous actors; some were uniquely skilled; some were top-grade workers who had worked at the Hanyang Arsenal making guns and cannon; there were others whose histories were by no means honourable but nevertheless fascinating. If you were to research these people's lives you could go back a century in time. But a cinematic technique such as the flashback is needed, for otherwise you would find it hard to believe that bent, wizened old lady with white hair once performed in *A Goddess Scatters Flowers*.

Summer is an outdoor time. After nightfall the stars hang down low above the lanes and a wind comes pouring in, brushing past the door of every home. This wind had a powerful attraction, for it drew out into the open all life hidden within the small front yards and receding courtyards. Small stools and rattan chairs were placed on either side of the lane and people would sit or lie there, receiving the benediction of the cool breeze. This was particularly true in those houses with entrances off the lanes and a common brick-floored area which served as an arena for enjoying the cool air and resting a while. Cold water was poured over the bricks and neighbouring families would congregate there. Even the old and bedridden were carried out by their grandsons in their rattan chairs to be greeted by their neighbours. Then all the secrets and gossip of ordinary people could be ferreted out here including discussions of oil, salt, firewood and rice, new daughters-in-law and daughters leaving home to get married — all became topics of conversation. Only the younger generation were more mobile: young friends would arrive and go off again in a group; then along would come someone in a dress who would stand at a distance beneath a streetlamp and beckon, and a rattan chair would creak as a young lad was enticed away. The young are reluctant to look back into the past too much, preferring to make more demands on the future, and those who demanded the most were not outside at all but facing their books, outlines or blueprints, interminably sweating within their rooms as they toiled away within the haze from mosquito coils.

Strangely enough, there are not so many people out in the lanes this summer taking advantage of the cool air — there is a tendency nowadays for the formerly outdoor life of summer to be concealed behind doors. The abominable television is the culprit, its popularity rising daily in leaps and bounds. Old and young alike gather together in dimly-lit rooms, every one of them silent and staring ahead as an electric fan turns round and round. Now you can have cool air and be entertained at the same time, so no one wants to go outside anymore. A diverting sight now is the keen amateur TV assembly-men, youths with dishevelled hair and untidy clothes who carry out already assembled TVs still lacking their frames, set them down on the ground and show off their technical wizardry, providing a free service to those who are not yet able to afford a TV or do not yet wish to buy one. And quite a few people sit around quietly, just as at an open-air film-show in the countryside.

The day's activities in these small lanes are wound up by the young. At the quietest time lovers come and go in the empty, silent lane, their footsteps matching in close, rhythmic harmony. During that season the streetlamps are very bright, reflecting off the whitewashed walls and turning the moon hanging above the lane a dark red shade. The footsteps halt, a key turns, the woman pushes open the door and enters; the man hesitates before leaving, turning to look back as he walks away; the closed door opens again and the woman leans far out to wave again and again — this couple is filled with love and understanding. There is something wrong with that couple, however, for the man seems at a loss and stands to one side while the woman, piqued and mortified, leans against the stone pillars of a memorial. Both seem stubbornly ready to wait for the moon to go down. Go home, young lady. It is cold and dewy outside and it is unwise to stay out too long. Nor can you rely on those stone pillars — they are just inert, unfeeling objects. . . .

When you are faced with a main thoroughfare you want to hurry; when faced with a mountain you want to climb it; when faced with the sea you want to sail far away. And what about when you are faced with deeply receding lanes such as these? Well, then you stroll along slowly, stroll past those high walls, stroll along over the small, broken cobble-stones, stroll along with your hand against the stone pillars of the memorial to give you support, go looking for art's realm, go exploring life's resources, listen carefully for history's echo . . . perhaps I have found something small which for the time being at least is recorded here and, while it may not seem like much, do not be impatient but let me continue to stroll along slowly. . . .

October 1983

Translated by Alison Bailey

梦中的天地
陆文夫
熊猫丛书
*
《中国文学》杂志社出版
（中国北京百万庄路24号）
中国国际图书贸易总公司发行
（中国国际书店）
外文印刷厂印刷
1986年第1版
编号：（英）2—916—34

¥10.00

UNIVERSITY OF CA., RIVERSIDE LIBRARY
3 1210 01056 6964